PRESENTS

THE EUROPA ASCENT

PATRICK LOVELAND

Copyright 2020 © Patrick Loveland
Published by: Darker Worlds Publishing
Edited by: Chad A. Clark

Darker Worlds logo design by:
PETER FRAIN
77studios
www.77studios.blogspot.com

Cover design by:
PATRICK LOVELAND

All rights reserved.

This book or any portion thereof may not be reproduced, copied, shared online, transmitted or used in any manner whatsoever without the express written permission of the author, Patrick Loveland. Quotations may be used for the purposes of a book review, so long as they are used with attribution.

This book is a work of fiction. All names and locations presented are solely the work of the author's imagination. Any resemblance to actual persons, events or locations is unintentional and coincidental.

ISBN — 9 7 8 - 1 - 7 3 3 3 3 4 9 - 3 - 8

For my father, who accidentally kick-started
my love of Sci-Fi/Horror. I miss you.
And my brother, for pouring fuel on that love's fire by
putting on movies in our room late at night that
I never should have been watching at that age.

ONE

Three overlapping cones of light flickered on, their hazy brilliance eating away at a vast expanse of inky, swirling darkness. Specks twinkled all around, then swirled and were swallowed by the darkness again as the source of luminosity moved through them and continued onward. Darkness reigned here. This light, like its source, was alien.

Sidd Priddy deftly manipulated dual control sticks, remotely maneuvering a submersible drone along an ocean floor of frost-strewn ice, miles below from a padded, reclining seat. Wisps of this agitated frost slid and whirled as the drone-sub glided along the hard, frozen surface. Sidd experienced this as a live three-dimensional feed through a visor placed over his forehead and eyes. Below the visor, he was smiling. Usually was.

A small gathering of station personnel—made up of project scientists and repair crew—viewed the same feed as a large, real-time diorama, hovering in the air near a curved wall of transparent plasteel. This soft-edged virtual portal into the drone's reality appeared as a shared hallucination through their standard issue Augmented Reality contact lenses. Like a floating, curved prism of teleported actuality. If asked, Sidd would have call this technology: "Nifty."

Next to Sidd sat Granger—first name Ed, but Sidd never called him that—fiddling with his own set of controls. Granger was a comms tech and the ears to Sidd's eyes on this duty. Right now, only the sounds of the drone's inner workings, the rush of water past its mics as it advanced, and the larger shifting of Europa's sub-surface ocean filled the facility.

Europa Station KC-3 was a cluster of layered, inverted domes built into the inner surface of the moon's outer ice crust layer, like a lamp on a section of its ocean's ceiling. This lamp arrangement was built around and over the bottom end of a miles-deep tunnel, bored down from Europa's icy outer surface.

This was the lowest part of the whole station, the nadir of the central structure's dome, and itself a much smaller inverted dome that bulged out of the larger one. The assembled team stood on a flat disc of more plasteel that had three rounded rectangle cutouts radiating from a central point—'moon pools' for drone egress and ingress, and hydraulic winches and cranes for help with maintenance.

Sidd liked to think of this level as a 'glass-bottomed boat' like he'd seen in an ancient Doris Day movie his grandfather watched on the vids. The whole outer structure of the station was plasteel, but this was the only place you could actually stand on it and look down. The ocean was so dark and lifeless he didn't think anyone other than bored scientists would pay to see down into it.

Sidd's drone was the only one in use, two more hanging in their hoisted and locked positions on cranes over sealed pool hatches. The drone crew wore puffy biosuits designed to combat cold and pressure—if they had cause to don helmets and climb out onto the station exterior for general maintenance—and stood waist-deep in the open moon pool, their boots hooked on a support rail that formed a ring around the pool's opening.

Khondji, a younger scientist, studied a readout that hovered in the air near him.

"From the rising temperature, we must be approaching some unrecorded hydrothermal venting points."

"Overlay thermal mesh, please," Hitomi Vanlint, the head scientist, said.

Granger pressed an AR button floating above his physical interface and the drone's feed displayed a subtle grid over the image, with shimmering colors representing different temperatures on the live image. "Thermal mesh active."

Sidd said, "Hey, you shouldn't distract the driver, pretty colors or not. Now if you wanna put on some good ol' country western music...."

Granger chuckled and said, "That's all you listen to, isn't it? Ancient country music, jangling away in the drill-trucks. I hear it in the background over comms."

"Not true, mate. I also listen to classic crooners, doo-wop... mariachi...rocksteady...taiko drums...."

Granger shook his head. "All at once?"

Khondji frowned. "Granger."

"Sorry."

Vanlint sighed. "And please remain professional, Mr. Priddy...."

Sidd said, "Will do..." then under his breath, "...but it's not like Geeky Pete's gonna find anything down here."

Vanlint glared at Priddy, not that he could see it. "What was that, Priddy?"

"Nothin'.... Just drivin'."

"Mmhm.... I know that's what you do. That's what you do so that we are able to do what we do. As you may have heard in rumors and speculations, Olatunji-Huang Heavy Industries now has its own research stations here. Langston Biotech, as well."

Khondji said, "They've cloaked their facilities and been quite discreet about making planetfall and supply deliveries, but we've been monitoring them."

"And not only are they here—they seem to have made some discoveries. Kintetsu Corporation cannot afford to fall behind any further."

Sidd sighed, still half-smiling. "Understood, ma'am."

"Fantastic. And please refrain from referring to the drone as 'Geeky Pete.'"

Sidd had to stifle a laugh at hearing Vanlint say the nickname he'd given the sub, even being as annoyed as he was.

Granger tapped away at his physical interface. Glowing letters appeared in the upper periphery of Sidd's AR overlay view, but not on the shared view the others saw.

DUSTY—CUT IT OUT

Sidd double-pressed a button on one of his control sticks and a tiny green signal light on a visible area of the drone body in the feed view blinked twice, in acknowledgement.

No one seemed to notice other than Granger, who chuckled softly before his face went slack and his eyes darted back and forth as he touched a couple fingers to one of his earphones.

"Hold it, Dusty."

"I'm almost to the hot spot...."

Vanlint said, "What is it, Granger?"

"I'm hearing what I'd expect to hear from a hydrothermal vent, dead ahead. We've examined a few, so I'm sure of that. But over this way..."

Granger activated a glowing icon on a taskbar on the AR feed lower edge, which also created a shifting, hazy circle to the left of the drone, in the distance.

"...there's something else I haven't heard on any of our first few missions down here. Actually, I've never heard anything quite like it, if I'm being honest."

Khondji said, "Can you boost it so we can hear it?"

"It's low and kind of subtle, but I can try."

Granger went between physical knobs and AR dials in his floating overlay, then pressed one last glowing button in the air in front of him. The sounds of the anomaly played over the regular sounds of Europa's sea. It was noisy, due to Granger boosting gain and other settings to make it more obvious, but definitely not his imagination. A low, rhythmic thumping with faster pulsing sounds in-between. Cardiac, almost.

Vanlint and Khondji shared a look.

Khondji said, "Excellent find," then to Sidd, "Priddy, discontinue current course and approach the area Granger has marked."

"Yessiree."

Sidd steered the drone toward the hazy glowing spot Granger had marked. As the drone came closer, the frost swirled more and there was a dense and darkening haze to the water in that direction, thickening as the drone drew closer.

Vanlint said, "Priddy, hold there."

Sidd eased the drone into a hovering stop over the icy sea floor.

"There seems to be a cloud of silt or some other detritus surrounding the anomalous area," Khondji said.

Vanlint brought a hand up to her chin and stroked it. "Probably from deep in the crust, below the ice, maybe making its way out of rifts, as we've seen with other vents. This is darker, though. The particles also seem to be...vibrating. As if it's affecting the water around it? Am I imagining that?"

Granger examined one of his readouts. "No, you're right. Something is definitely causing high levels of vibration, which seems connected to the sounds I picked up." He brought up the feed in his personal overlay and his eyes danced as he studied it. "And look—"

Granger manipulated the shared AR diorama, focusing on a smaller area of the particles in the water. In close-up, the shifting of the particles seemed less random. He made some adjustments and added a tilted cubic grid over the image, then tuned a few dials.

"The particles in the water are forming different, changing patterns based on the tones and frequencies the anomaly puts out."

Khondji raised his eyebrows. "Yes. Within each beat, rhythmic patterns, beat.... There are many patterns affecting each other within each pulse."

Vanlint said, "Return to the full image, please." Granger did as she asked. She frowned and pointed with a haptic-gloved hand of her own, a glowing circle appearing in the diorama near the sea floor. "What are those?"

Sidd feathered the drone thrusters forward.

Small patches of thin stalks sprouted from the ice, getting denser and more layered off into the murky distance. They swayed with the shifting currents like seagrass and caught the drone's lights with a strange iridescence.

Sidd hovered closely over a grouping of the wispy, blue-black growths. Granger zoomed in on the stalks, revealing tiny spherical nodules dotting many of them.

Khondji narrowed his eyes. "Are those organic?"

"It's difficult to say. We'll have to take samples after discovering the source of the vibrations. Priddy, continue on."

Sidd accelerated the drone smoothly forward.

"I'm gettin' some glare off the floatin' particles and weird grass. Switchin' to angled floor-facin' lights. Never thought I'd need these 'fog' lights down here." He switched to the sub's lower, smaller lights only, illuminating the sea floor ahead in a dimly glowing, flat cone. Shadows thrown forward from the stalks ahead made Sidd think of spider or insect legs.

"Yes, that's improved what little visibility there is. I am eager to see what could possibly be...." Vanlint trailed off, her mouth hanging open as her eyes darted around the AR feed display. She wasn't alone. Every eye in the room was locked on the AR feed now, many mouths agape like hers.

A large silhouette loomed in the haze of pulsing detritus ahead of the drone. Motionless and dark. Waiting.

Sidd lost his ever-present 'driving smile' and allowed the sub to slow, almost to a stop.

Vanlint said, "Keep going."

Sidd feathered the sub's thrust forward, creeping closer to the Stygian form. He noticed a growing distortion to the sound and image feeds that seemed to increase as the drone neared it.

It was taller than it was wide and made him think of old submerged shipwreck vids he'd seen. But as the shapes and surfaces that made up the thing became more visible through the dark haze around it, he realized how wrong he was. As the structure came into view, he eased off the drone thrusters again and let it hover in place.

Vanlint covered her open mouth as Khondji leaned forward,

both staring with wide-eyed amazement. One of the sub crew standing in the moon pool gasped, while another whistled.

"Dusty. What is that?" Granger said.

Sidd shook his visored head.

The thing rising from the seafloor was only dimly visible through the pulsing particles and bumpy stalks. The audio and visual feeds distorted more, adding a layer of noisy haze to the physically present murk around the thing.

The vertical structure that had initially struck Sidd as resembling a sunken ship was a roughly cylindrical tower. A rounded taper at the top rose from a more complex base structure. Billowing up out of the tower was a steady plume of churning black clouds that resembled smoke. A set of smaller, canted cylinders went around the tower's lowest area in a circular arrangement. Each was connected to the next by tubes, sprouting from their tops and to the tower base by sockets that their lower ends tapered down to. The rest of the base spread out asymmetrically to one side and was made up of many bulbous parts connected by ribbed conduits.

This thing gave Sidd the creeps.

Khondji cleared his throat and swallowed. "The structure definitely seems deliberately constructed and placed. Not random, as sunken debris might be. Are those some kind of...ruins?"

"Something like that," Vanlint said.

Granger made some adjustments on his overlay. "This structure is definitely the source of the sounds and patterned vibrations."

"Yes, my ears are still functional, Granger." She narrowed her eyes. "A machine of some kind?"

"Could be. Whatever it is, it's doing...something."

Khondji leaned closer to Vanlint and lowered his voice.

"I mean, is it possible that's a competing company's equipment?"

"Not a chance." Vanlint rubbed her chin. "Priddy, main lights back on and a bit closer please."

Sidd feathered forward and stopped again, then turned the layered cones of brighter light back on. Seeing the structure more clearly—combined with its low thumping pulse—twisted his stomach. It filled him with inexplicable dread.

The strange machine looked ancient, but not from rust. Sidd's gut feeling upon seeing it was that it was diseased. Decayed. The bumpy stalks nearest the machine had attached themselves in parts and clung like tendrils. Or, even more unsettling to him, looked like they could have grown out of its surface like swollen varicose veins. There were larger spheroid protrusions of varied sizes all over its structure and areas where those seemed to have eaten away at the surface, exposing unknowable inner workings. The machine had the appearance to him of something that had once been alive and become very sick. Cancerous. Consumed by uncontrolled growth. Then left to petrify. Only it still functioned, somehow.

"Incredible," Vanlint said.

Khondji nodded. "It truly is. I have to imagine whatever its purpose is, it seems to be powered by the hydrothermal vents it was built over."

"Or grown...."

"What was that, Priddy?"

"Just that it looks like somethin' that's...alive in some kinda way. Like it was alive, or still sorta is."

Khondji scoffed. "Preposterous—"

"No, Priddy might be more correct than we know. Possibly in a way we are unable to grasp. I will say with certainty that this is no human machine. I normally hesitate to use the term, but I believe this is something truly...alien."

"I can't disagree with that. I'm curious, though. Granger, please give me an acoustic sounding. I want to see how far down it goes."

Granger activated a sonar pulse and fed the resulting mesh of renderings over the AR diorama in real time.

"It appears to be installed in the ice at the top of what has to be an ancient fault or rift. That's what lets the hydrothermal venting to flow up into it and power it somehow."

Vanlint gestured, highlighting a section of the view below the main machine structure. "And what would you say that is?"

"Sonar can't effectively go through ice this thick... but it looks like there could be a subsection to the machine..."

"Radar, then. Low frequency."

Granger looked back at Vanlint. "How low?"

Sidd wanted to look and see if Granger was anywhere near as unsettled by all this as he was. Ten minutes before, he was sure the most they'd ever find here would be alien crabs or anemone around the vents. Something small and harmless. Nothing smart. Nothing scary.

Vanlint looked at Khondji. "One hundred thirty megahertz or thereabouts?"

"One-twenty on the lowest end and somewhere a little over two hundred should do it, I'd say."

Granger made the adjustments and activated his radar, the results adding and interlacing their own distinct mesh pattern and colors with the thermal and sonar info already on the real-time feed. The lower section previously obscured from sight by the ice now bloomed, growing in size and depth below the machine they could see at the surface. The vague mesh glow of the form was large enough that it brightened the room, then faded out some distance away all around.

Vanlint took a few steps forward, marveling at the feed diorama. "How did we miss this?"

"Maybe it's cloaked in some way, but only to our more advanced types of scanning."

"Make new friends, but keep the old...." Sidd half-sang.

Vanlint glared at Sidd, shook her head, and returned her focus to the feed.

Khondji crossed to Granger's station. "Is that all of it?"

"That's all it can pick up from here, radar being what it is. We could go around the area and keep adding to the saved mesh—"

Granger touched his headphone.

Khondji hovered behind Granger. "What is it?"

Granger made some adjustments and added a new amplified sound to the feed.

Sidd rotated the drone toward its source. "Is that...singin'?"

"Something like it, yeah," Granger replied.

Sidd adjusted and engaged the drone's thrusters, causing a

smooth ascent through the dark particle haze around the alien machine and a swirling of some of the taller detached bumpy stalks around it below.

"Gonna try to get eyes on whatever's making those sounds."

The water above the haze was still an inky black, but the tri-cone lights could illuminate a much larger area in front of the drone, again. The song-like sounds came closer. Then something floated down into the drone's lights and Sidd whistled out of astonishment.

"I guess I officially take back what I said earlier…"

A group of large sea creatures descended into view.

Graceful yet powerful. Bright orange. Fleshy 'beluga'-like rounded heads. Several cloudy half-dome eyes on each side of their almost obscenely layered folds of mouth tissue. Bulbous bodies that tapered toward the rear. Groupings of plumage, where more solid fins would be on Earth whales, seemed to do the same job—almost like enormous betta fish, Sidd thought. Whales and bettas were the closest things to these beings he'd seen—but even then, only in docu-vids of an Earth unlike the one he'd ever known. These creatures seemed similar, but Sidd figured he could be way off.

Vanlint's eyes widened. "Wondrous."

Sidd found these creatures far cuddlier than the machine below, so he accelerated toward them.

Vanlint grimaced. "You'll startle them."

Sidd shook his head. "Don't think so, ma'am. Seems like they're curious. Probably came after hearin' our sensor pulses."

The graceful behemoths glided closer to the drone.

Granger smiled. "Makes sense, yeah? Might've sounded like their own communications in a way."

Sidd nodded. "Exactly."

He feathered the thrusters toward them again, but this time they did retreat a bit, and layered sets of eyelids blinked over their big, cloudy eyes.

Vanlint frowned. "Either way, please switch to lowlight mode."

"Yes, ma'am." Sidd switched off all the lights on the drone and activated lowlight imaging. The feed displayed a muted greenish-blue. He scrunched his face up and raised a gloved hand to highlight some areas on a few of the largest creatures' bodies in the feed.

Concave absences of flesh.

"What do you make of that, though, y'all?"

"Burns?" suggested one of the techs from the moon pool.

Vanlint looked back at her, then at the feed again. "Yes, actually. Like gouges taken from their bodies, then cauterized...."

Khondji nodded, speechless.

Vanlint rubbed her chin again. "That machine and these creatures seem unrelated."

"Agreed," Khondji said.

"Suppose...."

"Yes?"

"Pure hypothesis, but...it's possible that an advanced lifeform had cause to use Europa's oceans as a kind of habitat."

Sidd looked over the bulky, fleshy creatures again. "Or maybe a farm?"

Vanlint looked at the simple-seeming, visor-wearing drone pilot again, this time with no disgust or judgement.

"That is also possible."

Then they heard it.

It was like a quavering or trilling sound.

Close enough that Granger didn't need to boost it.

This sound made Sidd's stomach twist even worse than the weird machine had done—and every time it sounded again, the distortions the alien structure emitted got stronger in wavering pulses.

The odd whales sang and moaned to each other, then swam off out of the lowlight view's periphery.

Escaping?

Only seconds later, dark, vague shapes made chase through the murky water, trilling all the way. They were far enough from the drone that even the lowlight mode barely picked them up—and there were enough of them trilling that the distortion on the visual feed from the alien machine below—that Sidd had decided was definitely reacting in some way to that awful, haunting sound that came out of them—made the creatures almost invisible.

These new creatures seemed to move through a kind of asymmetrical undulation. They tumbled through themselves like dough being kneaded, still somehow quite rapid and focused in their trajectory. Even when glimpsed through the fog of darkness and machine distortion, they were still difficult to get a good look at. Sidd couldn't tell if that was because of the water swirling around and through them during their strange motions, or something about the bodies themselves.

After both beasts were well out of sight and range of the sound pickups, all they heard was the shifting of Europa's seas and the eerie pulsing of the alien machine below.

"Fascinating. There really is so much more to study here," Vanlint said.

Khondji beamed at Vanlint. "As you've asserted many times."

Vanlint nodded. "Obviously there's a diverse biosystem, complete with a feeding chain and predation. Even more incredible.... Abandoned technology of what must have been an advanced civilization."

Sidd cleared his throat. "Please advise."

Vanlint winced. "Pardon?"

"These are real high priority discoveries. Incredible, sure...but also very possibly dangerous. Shouldn't we—"

"Ah, yes. I'd read about your history with anomalous lifeforms in your company file...."

Granger typed HUH? So that only Sidd saw it in his visor display. Sidd activated a tiny red light on the drone's body and Granger frowned.

"Rest assured that these findings will be thoroughly reported and discussed. I will call for an emergency meeting with on-station administration and Sol-Three corporate officials."

"Understood."

"And for now, place remote cameras in the ice around the visible upper area of the anomalous machine for observation. Also, a few more that observe the surrounding waters. Get a sample of the nodule-covered black sea grass, as well. Then bring the drone back and consider yourselves off duty and under a gag order. Same for you, drone team. Mention none of this. Do not discuss it, even with each other."

Sidd flexed his jaw muscles around clenched teeth.

"Yes, ma'am."

Vanlint lowered her voice and said to Khondji as they walked toward a thick traversal column in the center of the moon pool deck, "And I'll need my explorer unit prepared for use in the very near future...."

Granger typed, NICE JOB. REALLY WANTED TO BE ON HER BAD SIDE. BUT I GUESS YOU OWED ME A HAIRCUT AND WARP-PONG TOURNA-MENT ANYWAY

Sidd chuckled softly, then blinked the tiny green light on the drone body twice.

TWO

Sidd and Granger filled trays with food—which ranged from acceptable to almost delicious—from a curved wall of automatic vending panels in one of the station's mess halls. Specialized drones cooked and cleaned all around.

The hall itself ran along one of the outer rings of deck inside the station's central structure, an inverted half-capsule that the lamp domes radiated around. The moon pool and sub deck bulged down from the underside of the facility. The men dispensed their beverages and found an open table in the bustling eating area.

Sidd had replaced the sub's VR visor with his lucky hat—a mesh-back trucker style, with a CAT logo—short for Caterpillar Inc., a huge construction and spacefaring vehicle and equipment company. It was almost threadbare and even though it had faded from use, Granger had joked in the past about it being bright orange and camo at the same time. But Sidd knew why it was and didn't care what he said.

Sidd set down his tray and removed his hat to eat, tucking the mesh snap-back into the rubberized foam front panel and folding its bill to tuck it into his back pocket.

Granger looked at Sidd's stacked plate.

"You must have some high metabolism, man. You just eat and drink and eat some more? Then you gain, like, nothing? I gotta watch it or I get chubby."

"You're fine, mate. And me, I'm fixin' to pack it in 'cause my body thinks it's winter, from the cold," Sidd said, taking a big bite out of a meat-flavored protein bap.

"But it's not cold in the station."

Sidd finished chewing and swallowed. "Listen, Mr. Squawk Box.... You never have to work the drill-trucks, or the loadin' dock rigs. This luxurious temp regulation doesn't come on in there. The trucks only get minimum life sustainin' warmth 'cause the drills use so much power. You still gotta bundle up."

Granger shrugged. "Still sounds a little silly to me."

Sidd chuckled and shook his head. "I'll be sure to realprint a little clown hat with a string and wear that when we eat."

"Hey, the air regs up at the Lake go out sometimes, too. I'm not that spoiled."

Sidd frowned. "What do they do at the Lake, again?"

"They study chaos terrain formations and look for differences between the under-ice ocean vent formed ones and the...uh...well, lakes that form in the ice itself. The water differences too, if any."

"Well, I'll be.... Look at you, brainy."

Granger snorted as he dropped his fork onto the tray. "That exhausts my regurgitated paraphrasing of what one of the techs told me. Not something I could expand on."

"I get you," Sidd said, and chuckled as well.

They ate quietly until the comms tech got a conspiratorial look in his eyes and leaned in closer. Granger lowered his voice and said, "So, what do you think about all that shit we saw? The machines and the aliens—"

Sidd's eyes darted around the eating area. "We can't talk about that."

"Come on, it's just m—"

Sidd cut him off with a wave of his hand. "You've never been sat down and laid into over breakin' a gag. That's prison. Penal mining colonies. Maybe worse...."

Granger frowned and shook his head, silent as he continued eating. And as the silence began to stale, Sidd tried changing the subject.

"Hey, there's another reason I'm eatin' like I got a hollow leg...."

Granger looked up. "And what's that?"

Sidd lowered his voice as he said, "I gotta get a base goin' if I'm gonna get good and fucked up after this."

Granger raised his eyebrows. "Sloppy warp-pong?"

"You bet your ass—the sloppiest of warp-pongs."

"Sounds great, but you have to do my hair before you get too fucked up."

Sidd said, "Oh yeah, no problem. I like trimmin' you up."

THREE

Sidd's eyes danced over the familiar freckles on Granger's neck, where his old, but well-maintained hair clipper tool was buzzing as it trimmed the reddish-brown hairs on the back of the comms tech's head. There was an AR overlay faintly glowing on his head that was locked to his movements, a representation of what the final desired lengths would be based on the style he and Granger had agreed upon and keyed in.

They'd picked Granger's quarters as they were more spacious, and the rougher types who inhabited the tighter multi-bunk crew quarters didn't seem to like having Granger around the last time. Or maybe it was more about Sidd spending more time with him than them.

"...Wait, so your name is Ed E Granger? So, if you went by Eddy, you'd be Eddy E Granger?" he asked and chuckled.

"I guess—but my middle name is Ezekiel, which is pretty cool."

Sidd pulled the buzzing clippers away from Granger's head and laughed.

"That's worse! Eddy Eazy Granger."

Granger laughed and shook his head. "Hey, at least my name's not Sidd Priddy. That's a pretty cruel thing to name a boy."

Sidd sobered some. "Well, I mean...that's not exactly what they named me. And I doubt they meant for me to go by Sidd."

"Why? What's your middle name?"

"Which one...?"

Granger frowned. "Huh? What's your whole name then?"

Sidd went back to trimming.

"What's wrong?" Granger asked.

"Let's just say my heritage is multi-cultural."

"Nothing weird about that."

Sidd sighed. "My name is Siddhartha Junyi Priddy de Gonzalez."

"That...is...amazing."

"Shut up."

"No, I mean it. It's incredible. I'm still just going to call you Dusty, though. You understand. Actually, where'd the Dusty come from, then? And is all that heritage why you talk like a British cowboy?"

Sidd shook his head and grinned.

"Father was full-blooded Indian. He grew up goin' between Wales and Bangalore. Mother, Chinese and Guatamalan. I grew up in Swansea. Then they got divorced and I bounced all over between her places in Guatamala. He moved to Manchester, then mother to Panama, and my dad ended up in Texarkana, Arkansas in the US, of all places—"

Sidd nicked a tiny mole on the back of Granger's neck, making him flinch and gasp.

"Shit, sorry. Anyway, why Dusty? It's a long story and I'm not tellin' right now...so let's converse about somethin' else so I can finish," Sidd said as he continued trimming.

"Okay, okay. Just get me a medpack if the bleeding doesn't stop, all right?"

Sidd chuckled. "Sure thing. Hey, what about your big plan?"

"My plan? It probably sounds stupid...so don't tell anyone. I heard they found an Earth-like that's covered in archipelagos of beautiful islands. I just want to earn enough working these hazard pay level jobs to make it to that planet. Build a catamaran or some other boat like that and sail it from little island to little island."

Sidd smiled. "That sounds incredible. Am I invited?"

"Sure thing, man. Just a couple of buddies sailing around, fishing and drinking. Maybe special order shipments of rum to the next port to keep the stocks up and make some of those dumb Tiki drinks you talk about."

Sidd laughed. "Hey, they're tasty."

"I'll bet they are."

"Yeah. Just sailin' around. Couple of buddies...."

fOUR

Sidd and Granger stood on either side of a rec room ping-pong table, bent over and eyes locked as they gripped their paddles. Granger threw the ball up a few feet, then let it drop back—smacking it with his paddle, sending it arcing down toward the far side of the table—

But the velocity changed as it crossed over the table's edge, straightening its gentle arc, striking the flat surface, then cutting up away from it in almost a straight line at a twenty-degree angle. Paragrav took over again after it passed a few feet over the edge on Sidd's side, arcing down again, but from a higher point than it normally would—

Sidd smacked it back with some English on it, but as it went over the table, it lost the spinning arc, struck the surface, then shot toward Granger's side at an even more acutely angled straight line—

Granger let it come out from the table's influence and arc down before smacking it back—but it hit the net. Instead of rolling on the table it spun lazily over it, briefly floating up before being pulled down at a feather's pace. It made soft contact with the table again, then rotated slowly as it gradually ascended away.

They both let out drunken laughs and Sidd slapped the table, feeling the strange near weightlessness—and a slight vibration from its base being in a magnetic lockdown mode that was designed for unintentional grav loss.

"How's that for a comeback?"

Granger shook his head and said, "It's almost impossible to practice this silly ass game. There's no way to turn off the paragrav panels under the table uniformly, so every time we play, it's different."

"And that's why it's fun, man. It's fuckin' warp-pong, not some real competitive kind of thing. Not to mention downin' all that Kentucky contraband and that watered-down piss that the Kintetsu Corp has the stones to call beer.... We wouldn't be up for serious dealings anyway."

They laughed and the sound of it softly echoed off the walls of the curved recreation hall and its squat, non-regulation half basketball court, exercise equipment, and the other ping-pong table.

Sidd had found it funny that there was a half-court but not a basketball in sight, and even he knew the twelve-foot ceiling with a hoop and backboard right below it was way too low for normal play. Plus, the hoop had no net. It was when he was playing ping-pong one day when the basketball game started up.

There was no ball. They played with specialized haptic gloves and AR goggles, and from the way their hands jerked and slapped, they seemed to work well. The net-less hoop also glowed a little during play. Sidd figured the net was animated like the ball. He also imagined the players could see through the ceiling, a glowing scoreboard and shot clock impossibly high above. That way, the virtual ball wouldn't look strange sailing in arcs through the air that wasn't there.

He was just glad they had real ping-pong balls and paddles—so they could play this ridiculous variation of the game. There were haptic versions of it too, but they glitched enough that they kept the real thing for backup.

Sidd set his paddle down, watching it gently loll back and forth in slow-motion, then grabbed another beer from a little cooler tucked near one side of a curved inverted base that supported the table. He cracked it open—with the press of a button near the can's sealed mouth—and drank half of it in one pull.

Granger gestured for one. Sidd grabbed another can, but hesitated. He stepped back to his side of the table, whipped it around behind his back and let it go, the can wobbling around as it sailed smoothly through the low-G bubble over the table toward Granger's waiting hand. The beer passed the barely rotating ping-pong ball and it made Sidd think of a huge ship passing by a moon or small planet.

The comms tech caught the can, opened it, and took a sip.

"So...about before."

Sidd closed one eye and squinted at him. "Which before?"

"Vanlint said you had something in your file about—"

"Nah, I'm not supposed to talk about that, man."

Granger frowned. "What's the big issue? We're friends, right?"

"Damn straight," Sidd said, his gaze lingering on Granger's slick, freshly cut hair and bright, questioning eyes before looking away.

"Then what's the problem?"

Sidd drained his can and crumpled its woven biodegradable structure. "It's not up to me."

"Dusty, it's not like this place is bugged. I'm the comms guy, remember? If there were any weird little microphones and signals in here, I would've stumbled onto them. Same for AR mesh noise...."

Sidd studied Granger's eyes. "Well, if you ain't gonna leave well enough alone...."

"I ain't."

Sidd threw the crumpled can toward a recycling unit but it was low and bounced off. He grabbed another and opened it.

"There are a lot of things out here that they don't talk about."

Granger frowned. "Out here?"

"The frontier, man. Non-settled planets and moons, in our system and outside it. Even the settled ones have spooky shit they haven't figured out yet."

"I don't understand."

Sidd thought a moment. "Other than Earth, the Moon, and areas we've gone and settled on rocks we still haven't fully explored. We have no fuckin' idea what's out here. Took us this long just to get serious about Europa. Other than maybe its core, there's no resources that would've drawn us here before more recent alleviations of that need. Now it's more about discovery and knowledge and all that bullshit."

"Sidd, I know I'm a little drunk, but you're not making much sense—"

"You ever been out of the Sol system, Granger? Even once?"

Granger shook his head and sipped from his beer.

"Let's just say, while I was surprised that there was anything in this ocean at all, when I actually saw it, I wasn't all that shocked that some of it looked 'intelligently constructed'...or with how weird it all is."

"And why is that?"

Sidd sighed and thought another moment as the fizz of his beer blossomed up around him.

Then he pointed to his head and said, "All right, 'member how you were joshin' me about this hat?"

"You have to admit, it's pretty silly to have a bright fucking orange hat that's camo printed."

"Unless you're on Glamis-3...."

Granger's expression changed, his drunken playfulness vanishing.

"Glamis-3? What were you doing there?"

"Well, before I was driftin' around out here as basically a contract driver of whatever needed rollin' or flyin', I was in the United Sol System Merchant Marine. My ship was re-routed for auxiliary Naval duty."

"The Outpost Uprisings?"

Sidd nodded.

"I thought Glamis-3 was scorched. Some sort of chemical weapon the 'Posters had cooked up and lost control of."

Sidd shook his head. "Oh, it was scorched...but there was no chemical weapon."

"What was it?"

"You really can't repeat any of this...ever."

Granger raised his right hand. "I swear, Sidd."

He sipped and continued, "Okay, so I was drivin' in a convoy. It was a half dozen road trains—big truck in the front, several long trailer sections behind. Huge things, like fifty feet tall and wide, no tunnels to worry about fittin' into or bridges to go under, and such. And real long. Convoy probably stretched a couple miles. Military prefab structures, equipment, artillery, and one with personnel and their small arms. Auto-turrets all over the exterior of the whole length."

Granger nodded.

"One of our biggest ships made planetfall on the far side of the planet from the G3 outpost arcology. Harder to trace, they thought, even with all the scramblers and signal shields those big ships have. Not takin' chances, I guess. Then we were drivin' to a spot over halfway around from there. We were gonna set up one of the forward bases tasked with stompin' the G3 'Posters.

"Two other convoys were doing the same thing in other directions, plannin' for like a triangular pincer attack once we got to the other side. Glamis-3's huge. It was gonna take a while to get around, but once we all got where we were goin' and set up shop— they wouldn't have had a chance. I mean, it would've been a hell of a fight, but they couldn't have won it."

"Yeah, and...?"

"So, we're drivin' along across Glamis-3's legendary bright orange deserts, like Australia's outback on Earth but glowing some. And weirder plants here and there. Our uniform suits were camo like this hat, head-to-toe, and with internal air conditioning. The ones there to fight had sealed helmets and more armor. We had these hats and breathing masks with goggles that slotted in under 'em, for when we had to be out in the swirlin' dust."

Sidd finished his beer and set the empty can on the table. It wobbled lazily but did not fall down.

"Then we got caught in what seemed at first like a dust storm. It was to the sky, and howlin' like it was pissed-the-fuck off. And once it swallowed us, the glow from the sand was the only light. At first, they made us keep goin', but the sand messed up the bearings and guidance instruments too. We buckled down to wait it out...."

Granger squirmed in his seat at the extended pause. "What happened?"

"There were these...things in the storm."

"What things?"

Sidd winced. "I never saw one up close, and what I saw was hazy through the rushing wind and sand. They walked real strange, lopin' around. And they could jump up and float in the storm like they were in low-G—but Glamis-3 is almost Earth gravity. Anyway, didn't see 'em up close, thankfully."

"Could they have been from the outpost, people in special tactical suits or something?"

"No chance. I didn't have to see 'em clearly to know they weren't human."

"So what happened?"

Sidd sighed, eyes losing focus as his attention seemed to drift.

"Details don't matter...but those things.... They just killed everybody. Autoguns couldn't track 'em through the storm's whirlin' mess of particles. The soldiers were too slow and their guns and armor were nothin' to them. There were parts of troops everywhere in seconds, once the slaughter started. Then when the creatures knew they had taken us out, they started...eating."

Sidd grabbed another beer and cracked it. The metallic crack and fizzing of the contents served as the only sound as Granger pondered his retelling.

"How did you make it out?"

"I hid in my truck's cab at first, but I caught sight of them prying their way inside the next one in line over the AR link. I saw what they did to that driver, his AR mesh avatar just comin' apart. I put on my breather. Snuck out of the cab and slid slowly down the truck's access ladder to the ground, worried the sound of me clanking down forty or so feet worth of ladder rungs would attract those fuckin' monsters.

"Then I climbed up underneath my truck into one of the big tandem axel areas. I tucked in far enough that they just never saw me, I guess. A few even ran under where I was, but if I'm bein' honest, I shut my eyes every time and kinda...prayed, I guess. To what or to who, I couldn't say."

"Then what?"

"Storm passed. Monsters gone with it. Something about it killed the trucks too. Couldn't start even one up to save my life. I scavenged for some air tanks and filters...then water and rations, and started back toward the ship with a beacon pulsin' away. They found me a handful of days later, collapsed and unconscious in a swirling little dust devil. Like a baby tornado, I guess you could call it, just whippin' and whirlin' around me. So...there's your story behind the Dusty nick name, as a bonus."

"Damn, man. And yeah, I wondered why the other drivers called you that. So what happened to Glamis-3?"

Sidd sighed. "I was debriefed. They grilled me about the creatures. How they moved. How they...ate. Weapons? Armor? Told them the little bit of nothin' I told you, 'cause it's all I saw. Then I found out they'd lost the other two convoys too, only no survivors from those. Military didn't take kindly to losing all those people, equipment and resources.

"My ship moved on to a new auxiliary troop transport duty... and from what I heard, a few proper naval ships came in and glassed the whole fuckin' ball—outpost, creatures, everything. Some kind of orbital web array bombardment that just can't be legal outside of mining dead planets. So, I'm serious. Don't mention any of this, even hearsay as it is."

Sidd chuckled mirthlessly.

Granger shook his head. "Wow.... I hope that last part's not true, but mostly I'm just glad you made it out, Dusty."

"Shit—me too!" Sidd replied as they both laughed.

"Y'know, I figured out pretty quick—you're smarter than you come across."

Sidd raised his beer. "And twice as stubborn."

They laughed some more.

Granger said, "Also...mile-long truck-trains on Glamis-3? Dusty, is there anything you haven't driven or flown?"

"Hey, it's just what I do. Space, air, road, water—fuckin' ice now, on this job! I could do that dressage horse dancin' shit in a quadruped tank if you paid me enough. Hell, you don't even have to pay me if you catch me in the right mood!" Sidd said and they laughed hard.

"I will say I've been real curious about those huge combine harvesters that Olatunji-Huang has been usin' on...."

Sidd trailed off and Granger followed his gaze to the porthole window in a pressure door near the ping-pong table. There was movement in the connecting corridor—a ring of a wide, curving hallway that ran around the central structure's interior, connecting its outer sections that joined the outer domes with the inner operations areas and living spaces of central, where they stood.

Sidd said, "Unfuck the grav panels, man. Don't wanna get busted and written up again."

FIVE

Granger brought up a personal AR mesh interface and reset the paragrav panels to normal behavior, dropping the all-but-hovering ping-pong ball to the table. It bounced a few times before Sidd grabbed it and set it down, placing his paddle on top, resting at an angle.

Sidd could still see blurred movement out in the ring corridor, so he crossed over and peeked through the porthole. Armored security personnel—with STASEC glowing on their armor in AR—hustled down the hallway in two lines, side by side. There had to be twenty of them, most carrying shock-guns—but a couple of them had big auto-rifles. Whatever they had those for, Sidd hoped they'd been loaded with special rounds that couldn't go through or crack the station's plasteel exteriors.

Granger came up and looked out past him, the comm tech's chest brushing against Sidd's shoulder and his breath warm on his ear. "What's going on?"

Sidd said, "No idea.... Somethin's got Stayseck riled up." then pressed a contact pad on the door. It slid away and they stepped out as the last of the armed security detail disappeared around a junction corner.

The corridor walkway was flanked on both sides by curving rows of Breathing Trees™ in tasteful uniform pots, which were smaller than a very young regular tree but larger than most bonsai. They were about Sidd's shoulder level, resembling maple bonsai, and had been specially bred to produce even more oxygen for air production, with the help of artificial photosynthesis from finely tuned accompanying ceiling lights. There was a psychological benefit as well, which Sidd could attest to.

"Looks like they're goin' to the main elevators."

Sidd kept walking toward the junction and Granger followed. As they reached the corner of the intersecting corridor, they heard laughter past it. He looked toward it and saw they were being observed.

Two of the younger scientists who'd been in the moon pool dome earlier with them—Thomson and Asaaluk—were cracking up from watching them. Thomson clapped his hands in mock applause.

Sidd frowned at them. "What?"

Asaaluk smiled and shook her head. "You two are obviously inebriated. You carry it better than Granger, for the record. But you are drunk and creeping around looking frightened. It's comical."

"Yeah, what's got you looking so concerned?" Thomson asked.

"You guys didn't see Staysec marchin' past here, armed to the teeth?"

Asaaluk said, "Sure, but they're probably just breaking up a big fight in one of the idiot maintenance and drill-trucker bars." She cringed. "Sorry, Sidd. You're just not like most of them, so I forget."

Sidd ignored her and looked down the corridor that the security force had taken—in time to see the last of them packing into the station's big central equipment and supply moving elevator.

The freight elevator was a circular platform in a larger circular elevator access chamber, the platform surface about twenty feet in diameter to the chamber's thirty—with smaller personnel elevators at four points around the platform's outer ring, that Sidd thought looked like unneeded support pillars. There were smaller versions of this multi-elevator setup in the outer domes too, but this was the only one that could go all the way from Sub-level 1—a huge equipment and vehicle covered disc of a loading dock at the base of the miles-deep shaft descending from the sub-surface 'Plug' base—all the way down to the moon pools.

The doors closed vertically, coming together at about average chest level of the sec team, and from a display above the big elevator, Sidd saw that it was descending. He started down toward the elevators—

"Hey, Priddy—hold up!"

Sidd froze, then leaned to look back down the curved ring hallway.

Ojeda, a tall, stocky woman approached. STASEC glowed over her chest too, but instead of armor she wore a thick thermal jumpsuit with a holstered shock-pistol. She brought up a gloved hand that glowed then strobed, its light reflecting off Sidd and Granger's eyes and causing them to blink a few times.

"You guys are drunk again? I told you, if you're going to get so tipsy, you can't be stumbling around in common areas. I'm trying to be cool about it...."

Granger said, "They still have you busted down to mall cop duty?"

"What's a mall cop? You know what, never mind. Can you two just get back to—"

"Where are the rest of your buddies goin'?" Sidd said, pointing toward the elevators.

Ojeda clenched her jaw. "What buddies?"

"Like, two dozen security troops all armored up, and ready for war."

Thomson nodded. "He's right. Probably nothing, though."

Now Ojeda looked curious. She stepped into the connecting corridor with the elevators at the end and watched the display above the closed doors.

Sidd watched the sublevel numbers pulse, replacing each other as the elevator descended.

"That's the last level there's a bar on, or anything like that...."

They all watched it keep going until it stopped on the last one it could: DIVE BAYS

Granger touched Sidd's shoulder with the back of his hand. "That's the moon pools...."

Sidd shook his head slowly. "I don't like that at all."

Ojeda opened her comms. "Central, this is Ojeda. Can I get an update on a possible disturbance on the moon pool level? Some station personnel just saw a big sec team heading in that—"

Her eyes went back and forth, listening to tiny earpieces, Sidd assumed—as was standard for Kintetsu Corp. employees, and pretty much all offworld workers, nowadays. From her expression, Central's reply must have been pretty salty.

Ojeda winced, then frowned, but tried to recover her composure. "Not the concern of my post."

"So, like...need to know?" Granger said.

She nodded, staring at the elevator level display.

Sidd scoffed and started toward the elevators. "We're all in this station, so we all need to know."

Ojeda's right hand went to her shock-pistol's grip. "Priddy, stop."

He kept walking.

"Sidd," she said.

Sidd stopped and looked back. "Listen, it probably is nothin'. I'm just gonna go down there and sneak a peek. And I've got clearance still from steerin' a drone around earlier 'cause they might need me to do some more—so it's not against regs. You're in the clear."

Ojeda frowned. "Earlier?"

Asaaluk said, "That's correct, actually. We all have clearance from an earlier scientific mission that we can't discuss—Vanlint's orders."

"Yeah, you're good, Ojeda. Nothing to see here," Granger said and started toward the elevators, Asaaluk following.

Ojeda narrowed her eyes. "Vanlint herself?"

Sidd nodded and raised his right hand. "That's the honest truth."

Ojeda sighed and took her hand off her pistol. "You're lucky I like you, Sidd."

"Well, I mean...doesn't everybody?" Sidd scoffed, then continued to the closest of the smaller 'column' elevators, pressing a floating AR button to call it.

She chuckled and started toward them. "It would be irresponsible to allow you to endanger yourselves, clearance or not."

Asaaluk saw Thomson fidgeting in place back at the corridor junction.

"Come with us. Aren't you curious?"

Thomson scrunched his face up. "To a fault. But you saw what was...."

"There's a small army down there. We'll be fine," Asaaluk said.

Thomson nodded, then hurried down the corridor to join Asaaluk and the rest on the elevator.

Sidd keyed the lowest level and they started down.

SIX

Ojeda looked sideways at Granger. "So, what exactly is a mall cop, anyway?"

Granger smiled, his buzz showing. "Okay, so, I was watching some old sim-vids in the archives and in some there are these security guards that would roam around shopping complexes."

"We still have that," Ojeda said, frowning.

"No, these were people, not drones. And instead of responding to actual problems like theft and social unrest, they mostly just harassed customers."

Ojeda nodded but narrowed her eyes at Granger.

"If the consumers didn't seem like they were going to spend enough, the mall cops would make them leave. They even rode around on gyroscopically stabilized vehicles to be more efficient in their harassment duties."

Ojeda scrunched her face up. "Wait—that's what you called me? Prick."

Sidd chuckled and shook his head, thankful for any distraction from the dread twisting in his stomach as he watched the levels fly by on the display. He caught Asaaluk giving him a quick sideways glance and a smile, and wondered if she knew how much better a fit Thomson would be for her, if she were interested in him. Funny how that worked, Sidd thought, watching Granger verbally toy with Ojeda and admiring the mischievous, inebriated gleam in his eyes—

Sidd raised his hand. "Quiet down, y'all...."

He'd heard sounds from below. There, again—bursts of gunfire—

Gunfire and screams.

After a moment, the muffled cacophony was silenced—then replaced by the moaning of metal bending. What followed sounded like slapping, sliding, and climbing in the elevator shaft tube. The lights also glitched and nearly cut out completely. The sounds were quick and hard to make out, as they were still descending fast—to Sidd it was like something climbing, and he shuddered.

And he could have sworn he heard more muffled screams moving along with whatever was climbing up the shaft.

He brought a hand near glowing AR buttons hovering over the elevator command panel and pressed STOP—but smaller alerts faded up over his fingers each time he pressed it:

ERROR-DOCKING

"Shit! We missed the last braking junction...."

They all looked at each other with wide eyes.

Granger swallowed hard. "I was just kidding with you about the mall cop thing, Ojeda. Can you please get that shock-gun ready?"

Ojeda did just that, pulling her energy pistol out and aiming it at the doors as the elevator slid down to its last stop. It docked, clamps locking in, and the doors slid open.

The only lights were from their elevator interior and a glow from the exterior floodlights, shining in through the transparent plasteel and causing a bluish-green shimmering effect on the corridor wall. In the dim, limited glow, the smell hit them first, a rushing, cloudy wall of mixed sources. Gunfire, shock residue, possible bodily excretions—but mostly, brine. Pungent, funky saltiness overpowered every other scent, itself mixed with something acrid that struck Sidd as bile-like—post-vomit acid, not meant to be outside the stomach.

The elevator landing was a disc platform with six depressions around its edge that curved down away from the surface into channel-flanked, impossible-looking walkways. The platform surface was covered in layered slimy trails and puddles—some had blood mixed in, and piles of what looked like ground meat.

Asaaluk squeaked at the sight. "Can we just go back up?"

Ojeda put a finger to her own mouth to quiet her, and listened. "I don't hear anything down here."

Sidd nodded. "Yeah, sounds like whatever it was went up."

The momentary relief of that thought gave way to a flood of dread at the realization that up was where every other (Kintetsu Corp. employed) human on Europa was, not to mention their only isolated connections to civilization.

Thomson was shaking against the elevator wall. "What about Stasec?"

Ojeda tried to reach them on comms but got nothing.

Sidd looked through the transparent wall of the elevator tube and saw the freight platform was still in place where the station security troops had arrived—also covered in slimy blood trails and puddles.

He could just make out several large rents where the freight elevator's upper disc met its shaft tube's surface, the torn and bent openings all oozing even more glistening filth than the platform.

"I...don't think they.... I think we're alone."

Granger said, "What could do that?"

Ojeda shook her head. "I don't know.... O-H Heavy Industries hostile takeover squad with weird diving tech? Even Langston has used those kinds of teams, I've heard."

Asaaluk swallowed hard. "What about p-pirates?"

"There's not enough guaranteed payoff for pirates to operate on Europa. Takes too much overhead. Too dangerous. Plus, they'd need high level intel to even have a whiff of anyone being here."

"But what about that goo?" Granger asked.

Sidd looked at him but didn't say what he was thinking. He

left the elevator and crossed to the platform controls. Keyed it to climb several levels. It started up, taking the fetid bloody slime and accessible tears in its upper section with it.

Granger started, "What...?" but could see from Sidd's face there was no arguing. Instinct.

Ojeda caught the vibe, even if she didn't fully understand, and eased forward into a semi-crouched, advancing posture toward the edge of the elevator platform.

"I'm gonna check it out—"

"Are you fucking insane?" Thomson cried out, eyes bulging.

"Shut up."

Ojeda advanced with at least the appearance of confidence while most of the others looked on from inside the elevator.

Sidd's stomach twisted until it ached. He'd had a hell of a time getting himself to go back off-planet after Glamis-3. He was starting to seriously doubt his decision to join the ranks of the spacefaring again, one that he'd been so proud of at the time.

Ojeda crossed the landing and stopped near one of the channels that curved down and away from the surface, starting between one of several gaps in a ring of yellow-and-black-striped safety handrails that jutted up from the edge of the circle.

The station engineers had been creative down here with paragrav and chamber design. The panels on the curving floor of the channels kept you upright, as if you were on a flat surface. You walked down the curve and it kept you perpendicular to its surface. All of the curving parts met with a central column that descended away from the underside of the deck they stood on, running fifty feet to the moon pool level surface—where the shaft spread outward, smoothly curving as it connected with the deck. There were even integrated tracks between the paths for hauling equipment down the column.

Ojeda tapped her jumpsuit chest near her right shoulder and a small disc popped out from its surface. It detached, angled up a bit, and started whirring—a small drone. It climbed about a foot above her head and seemed to lock in place over the shoulder of her pistol-holding arm, emitting a cone of pulsing light. Sidd had seen these before, a cross between a combat flashlight and sensor.

She turned back toward Sidd by the freight platform shaft's "door," and the rest in the smaller elevator that seemed to grow out of it—the light-drone tracking along with her head movements and rotating around too.

"Going down. Anybody else?"

Sidd started toward her. Granger looked back and forth before following.

Thomson scoffed. "What are you people thinking?"

Sidd said, "She's the only one packin' down here...."

"Packing?"

Asaaluk started after the others. "I think he means the gun, and I can't argue with that."

Ojeda crossed to the closest flanked paragrav path and tested if it was still functional by holding a striped railing with her free hand and trying to step forward without dropping. It worked, so she kept going.

Sidd and Granger followed, then Asaaluk—but Thomson stayed frozen in the open elevator.

Sidd had never really gotten used to the transition hump of the paragrav channel from the elevator platform onto the column itself. You just kept walking down the path and it felt normal enough, but there was always a moment of panic where he just knew he was going to fall forward and drop to the moon pool deck below, dead—but he never did. You smoothly went from the platform surface around the hump to the column surface, a 90° change of angle.

In the dim light outside of Ojeda's pulsing cone, walking down the central column felt like approaching a large, circular wall.

Sidd could see the faint glow of two of the three moon pools from the side they came down—and that they were still open. The drones had returned and were secured to their maintenance cranes, but they were damaged. The swiveling arms of the cranes—used to hold the subs up and remove them from the pools when needed—were bent away from their intended operational position.

Ojeda looked toward the pool on their left, her drone's light washing over it as it pulsed.

"It looks like something...forced its way in...wrenching the subs out of the way."

Sidd had a worsening suspicion that he knew exactly what had caused all of this, but he tried to fight it off. He just couldn't think of what else it could be. The others who'd been here earlier with Vanlint's team—Granger, Asaaluk, Thomson—must have suspected the same.

As they approached the floor level, Ojeda's light burned through the inky dark, filling in the vague silhouettes ahead.

Glistening streaks of the briny muck and blood. Overturned equipment. Some thickly padded maintenance diving suits—for use while working on the station's exterior—had been torn away from their racks along the curved interior walls. The suits looked torn and possibly...melted, Sidd thought.

Ojeda crept down the curving slope that smoothly dovetailed with the dive level deck into a circular spread as it connected all around the central column.

To the rest of them, she appeared to be climbing the wall, impossibly. Then Sidd and Granger followed her down off the column, onto the deck and stayed close.

Granger unzipped a pouch near one of his jumpsuit's shoulder sections, took out a tube filled with murky fluid and bent it with both hands until it cracked loudly. He shook it up, causing it to glow a pale, bluish green. Chemlights. Sidd had forgotten that all their standard issue jumpsuits had this little backup safety feature. When Granger slipped his thick light back into its pouch, it glowed through the now-transparent material it had been stored in.

Sidd looked away from Ojeda's light and let his eyes adjust to the more subtle glow from the chemlight. The silhouettes took on more definition and he could see terminals and equipment, some also damaged and everything covered in the bloody slime.

Ojeda turned her attention toward him and everything outside of her cone of light went blank and vague again.

"What's down there?" Thomson whispered from above, by the edge of the platform, leaning over one of the railings to the side of a paragrav path channel.

Ojeda cringed and jerked her head up, light following and illuminating Thomson from below.

"Quiet!"

Granger scoffed. "Yeah, yelling that at him makes a lot of sense."

"Shut up, Granger. Or you might be subjected to my...harassment duties."

"Hey, you're the one who asked me to explain what I—"

"What is that...?" Asaaluk said.

Ojeda ignored her and scowled. "But you meant what you meant...."

"What? What does that mean?" Granger asked, screwing his face up.

Sidd shook his head. "Hey, at least Thomson made it out of the damn elevator."

"H-hey, what is that?" Asaaluk repeated, still standing on the central column. Sidd stopped and looked back at her. With her glinting eyes wide, she raised a shaking hand and pointed toward a few of the dive suits that were still on their racks.

Sidd heard it now—a light shuffling.

And something else.

Ojeda looked toward the suits and her light caught up. The suits were almost still, but shifting intermittently. She aimed her shock-pistol at them and practically tip-toed across the deck, stopping a handful of steps away. She gestured for Sidd and Granger to pull the suits away but they just looked at each other, then back at her. She motioned again with a stern glare.

Sidd didn't like it but sneaked over to one side, Granger on the other. Sidd looked back and saw that Asaaluk had backed halfway up the central column. She looked like a vampire or something to Sidd, looming above—and parallel to the floor, by their orientation.

He focused on the thick suits again, then Granger. They looked back at Ojeda and they all shared a nod. Sidd and Granger pulled the suits away and stretched back as far as they could—

A voice from between the suits cried, "No!" followed by a burst of auto-rifle fire—

Ojeda dropped to the deck and fired her shock-gun toward the flashes.

Sidd and Granger let go and threw themselves away to each side, allowing the suits to swing back together.

The colliding suits muffled a strangled cry, then there was silence.

SEVEN

Ojeda hauled herself to her feet and examined the singed fabric of her suit's left shoulder.

"Damn! Almost got me...."

Sidd got up and started detaching the dive suits that were obscuring their attacker, Granger following his lead.

It was one of the armored Stasec team troops. Ojeda's bolt had knocked them out. Their name display read: BIDDLE

Sidd had no intention of being shot at again and took the auto-rifle out of the troop's hands. There was a slight vibration running through the gun as he held it, and when his finger got close to the trigger guard, it started flashing a warning diorama in the AR overlay just above its carry handle—a looping three-dimensional animation of a vague human form being X-ed out as it picked up a gun-shaped object, and the words:

UNAUTHORIZED HANDLING OF STASEC WEAPONRY—SET WEAPON DOWN AND BACK AWAY

"You're kiddin' me, right?" Sidd said, but he'd already waited too long—

The auto-rifle's surface strobed with a bright pattern and shocked him with electricity, causing him to drop the gun to the deck with a loud clattering sound.

Asaaluk shrieked.

Thomson gasped above. "What are you doing?"

Sidd kicked the rifle away across the deck as he waved his pulsing, half-numb hands.

"Jesus, Thomson—shut up!"

Granger dropped the last of the puffy suits then looked over at Ojeda.

"You all right?"

"Yeah, just grazed. That could've been really bad."

Sidd crossed to Biddle, crumpled where the dive deck met the inverted dome's interior, felt for a node along the opaque helmet's jawline, found it and pressed. The helmet broke apart and collapsed into a compartment behind Biddle's sweat-covered, crew-cut head. His eyes fluttered behind shut lids. But he was still breathing—

Biddle's eyes snapped open and he came-to yelling incoherently—

"Fugckwherearethey—nnhhrun! Run!"

—and swung his arms around—until Sidd seized them.

"You're okay! It's okay!"

Biddle looked around then locked gazes with Sidd but his expression was wild. Face drained pale, skin almost the same color as the whites of his eyes.

"Fuck you it's okay! You didn't see them!"

Ojeda half raised her pistol. "See who?"

"Not who! They were sea c-creatures or something! But more like...fucking monsters! Took the whole team down like—" His voice caught in his throat and the look in his eyes changed to something more like haunted astonishment. "Like we were nothing...."

Sidd and Granger locked eyes.

Up in her paragrav vampire's perch Asaaluk said, "Oh my God...."

Ojeda shook her head. "What's he talking about?"

Sidd looked at the drone-subs in their bent cranes and closed his eyes. "They followed the subs back up...."

"What followed the subs, Priddy?"

Biddle gibbered—"They moved so wrong—and I couldn't even focus on them! Like they were blurry or something...."

Granger cringed. "You really think it was those things?"

Sidd nodded. "Has to be. Biddle, where's the rest of your team? Where are the bodies?"

"They took them! In their own b-bodies...." Biddle looked like he had meant to say more but trailed off, eyes darting around as his memory consumed him.

Sidd didn't like the sound of that or the look in Biddle's eyes.

"What's happening?" Thomson asked from above.

Asaaluk turned and looked up at him on the elevator platform. "Those ocean animals are in the s-station!"

Ojeda stomped her boot on the deck. "What is in the station?!"

Sidd stood up and locked eyes with her. "We were down here earlier with Vanlint and the most important science and corporate admin people on station. Granger and I guided a drone down to the sea floor. Way down...."

Ojeda narrowed her eyes and frowned.

"There are...machines down there. Not human-made. Then we saw some sort of alien whales...."

Granger sighed. "These other things chased the whales away. We didn't get a good look at them. Sounds like we wouldn't be able to anyway. Also seemed like maybe the creatures had some connection to the machines. But not necessarily in an intelligent way."

Sidd closed his eyes. "They followed our drone back up. The drone crew was s'posed to close the moon pools...."

Biddle freed an arm and grabbed one of Sidd's sleeves.

"You brought those fucking things up here?!"

Sidd wrested Biddle's hand off and let go of him as he stood. "Wasn't my goddamn idea, asshole."

Ojeda shook her head. "You're not kidding? You found deadly sea life in Europa's waters...and just let the station go on about its business? I'm just eating pea soup with some hot sauce and reading about overlay celebs an hour ago. No mention of fucking monsters in the water to distract me."

Sidd stared at her. "Yeah, boo-fuckin'-hoo. That choice to disclose is above my paygrade, all right?"

"Oh, workin' man woe-is-me is your take on this? I really misjudged you, Sidd. Thought you were a—"

"Ojeda, you don't know me that well."

"I guess you're right about that."

Granger shook his head. "Hey, maybe we should try to focus on the actual problem. How does that sound?"

Ojeda looked away from Sidd and scanned around with her synched hover-drone light, gripping her pistol.

She tried her comms channel again but got no response, frowning and cursing.

Granger turned to look. "What?"

"It's like there's some kind of interference. I can hear something...but it's like chopped up gibberish."

Something in her pulsing cone of light caught Sidd's eye—one of the drones hanging in a harness at an odd angle from its bent crane arm.

Sidd crossed to it. "Hey, swing the light back this way."

Ojeda looked back at him, so the drone did so without any effort on her part.

He examined the sub and rig, then grabbed one of the maintenance dive suits off the deck and put it on up to his waist.

"We need to know what's goin' on up there. How bad it is."

Granger nodded and grabbed a suit for himself. "Right...I get you." Once he had his suit half on and its over-boots on around his own, he joined Sidd.

They heaved the sub back toward the open moon pool.

"It's very fucking bad, I promise you that!" Biddle said.

"Jesus, Man. Did you just learn about the F word this mornin'? Switch it up a bit—and hey, your gun's over there, Spunky." Sidd pointed toward where he'd kicked the auto-rifle. "Since you're the only one who can pick it up, make yourself useful and cover Ojeda's ass, yeah?"

Ojeda and Sidd shared a look and nodded, her mouth curling just a bit at the edges of acknowledgement of his possible olive branch.

Then Sidd focused on the sub again, he and Granger lining it up as best they could over the moon pool. They climbed halfway into it, hooking the arches of their outer boots on the bent exterior ring of plasteel bar that descended into the water—held there in place by telescoping support struts that extended when a pool was opened. Sidd tried his best to "zen out" the images of blurry, shape-shifting sea monsters rushing up out of the dark water to grab him.

He stretched to activate the crane's AR joystick style controller. Through his feedback gloves, it felt like he had a narrow shaft of strong plastic or metal in his hand as he manipulated it. He tilted it, lowering the sub into the pool. Once it was completely submerged, he keyed a command to release it from the crane's grip. It bobbed in the water for a bit before auto-stabilizing jets kicked on in its roughly capsule-shaped hull, its rear/aft end sprouting the shrouded main propellers.

Biddle took Sidd's advice and retrieved his auto-rifle, any reluctance seeming to be pushed aside by fear of not having it. After hefting it in his hands, his panic seemed to lessen as his training kicked back in. Still strung out and wide-eyed, but scanning for threats—mostly up toward the elevator platform deck—gun at the ready.

Ojeda covered the moon pool as Sidd and Granger climbed out, then rotated the crane away. Granger keyed the moon pool hatch to close and it slid out of its storage area and across the surface of the water, almost flush with the surface, then sealed with a hiss and thunk.

Sidd and Granger crossed to the stations they'd used earlier that day, Sidd putting on his visor and Granger warming up his observation systems.

The AR motion diorama faded up near them, showing mostly darkness and glimpses of swirling water, bubbles seeming to float up toward the ceiling before reaching the top curving edge of the projection and disappearing.

Ojeda pressed an AR button on her chest near where her scanner drone had come from and its light went out. It hovered and tracked her head movement, at the ready if needed.

He maneuvered the drone around and tilted it up, revealing the eight glowing domes of the station. All surrounded by a dim haze from the interior lights spilling out of the transparent dome walls—before being swallowed by the inky black sea. The closest and smallest of them was the one that the drone had just left, the largest being the central dome that continued up to the surface—and large enough that it partially obscured the six lesser domes around it that were anchored to the ocean's ceiling of ice.

Long, narrow shafts of dark plasteel stretched between the main dome and the lesser six, and from each of these to each other. Maintenance and emergency tunnels he'd never had to use. "Finger cuffs" he'd always thought of them as, because each end's mouth had a set of robotic rollers that could move them to different connecting ports on the dome surfaces. Depending on the angle between the two, the tunnels would grow longer or draw shorter, accordian style, hence—finger cuffs.

All other station inter-dome transit was done through the upper levels of the domes just under the ice and through connecting corridors in the central inverted dome. Something to do with needing a way to seal off domes and sections from each other for any number of reasons that Sidd couldn't recall just then.

Most of the staff and crew just went to the outer domes for their work shifts anyway, spending off-time in the central structure.

The moon pool dome didn't have those because the curvature of the huge central dome obscured it from line-of-sight and connection, something Sidd had never thought about before–but wished was different at that moment.

Sidd maneuvered the drone into an arcing ascent, pacing the distance and angle to match the curve of the main facility structure's inverted dome shape.

As it rose in the water, they could see into the lab, barracks, corridors, etc. The ascent was rapid enough that they were just quick glimpses. There were a lot more darker areas than he would have expected, but no sign of the creatures—

Asaaluk let out a sharp gasp, close enough that Sidd realized she'd come down off the central column pathway.

Sidd slowed the sub to a hover. "What?"

"Look down and to the left...."

He brought the sub down and studied the corridors and intersections that stretched into the distance toward the station's central areas.

"There!" she said, and Sidd flipped his visor up on a swiveling hinge so he could see. The young woman's shaking hand pointed at something down a corridor the drone's camera was roughly aimed toward.

Then he heard a sharp intake of breath above. Thomson was also watching the diorama projection from the platform, hands tightly gripping the safety railing.

Sidd looked back at the drone feed and zoomed in.

There were a few station personnel running toward the drone's view, with the corridor lights flickering and cutting out behind them. Large, shifting shapes tumbled through the darkness on their trail, but he couldn't see anything clearly.

One of the escaping crew stumbled and collapsed as the others ran on. The lights glitched and shut off in the section the fallen crew member was in and they must have screamed, because the others slowed to look back—but the lights cut out again, quickly coming toward them and they bolted around a corner, out of sight.

Then the lights in that corridor junction cut out and the drone caught vague glimpses of one of the creatures, climbing across the darkened ceiling, lit up by the faint glow of the corridor the crew had escaped down.

It was all a chaotic blur of undulating movement.

Then those lights cut out too and all they saw was the corridor the drone was peering down abruptly ending in a wall of inky black.

After a long moment of just staring into the darkness and feeling his stomach twist into itself, Sidd backed the drone up and away from the surface of the dome. He noticed a tremor in his hands as he had the drone strafe from right to left, getting a view of different corridors and chambers with their darkened sections and personnel running or trying to barricade doorways with plasteel encased furniture and equipment.

Sidd shook his head. "How many are there?"

"There had to be dozens!" Biddle blurted out.

Ojeda cringed. "And how can they do that? Why do they look all blurry, and mess up lights and radios and all that? I mean, what are they?"

"The machine did somethin' similar. Lots of distortion around it—maybe being around it caused them to change."

"What do you mean?"

Granger nodded, thankful for the distraction, Sidd felt.

"Yeah, I think he's saying that the machine is pumping out some kind of field or something, like radiation. And maybe they were infected by it?"

Sidd nodded too, "Or maybe they live in it—you saw how big it was."

"Maybe, yeah."

Biddle let out a strangled chuckle. "Who gives a fuck?"

Asaaluk shook her head. "Don't they teach you soldier types to know your enemy? To help defeat them?"

"They trained us to fight people, not shit like this!"

Ojeda scoffed. "Maybe you just weren't paying attention, Biddle."

"Hey, at least I didn't get busted down to hall monitor for insubordination!"

"You know what, you cowardly piece of shit? You can go fuck yourself—"

A low whirring sound began on the elevator platform and they all jolted at once. Ojeda and Biddle aimed up toward it and she toggled her drone's pulsing light to come back on.

Thomson was gone.

Sidd engaged the drone's AUTO-STABILIZE setting and it "anchored" itself, its feed displaying a wobbling view of the central anterior dome as its thrusters intermittently fought the rolling currents to correct its position. Then he got out of the control seat and looked up.

"Thomson?" Ojeda called up—

The scientist slammed into the railing—startling them all again—but he just gripped it, wide eyes glinting and burning down into them in Ojeda's light.

"The freight elevator—the one those things climbed up out of? It's coming back down!"

EIGHT

It only really hit Sidd at that moment that they had no other way out of the moon pool lab. The rest of the facility was becoming an abattoir, sure—but they'd have to go up into it to be in real trouble.

They'd trapped themselves down there.

Ojeda started toward the central column. "Biddle—on me."

"You're not in charge! You don't even outrank me!"

She stopped to glare at him. "Trade me guns then, tough guy?"

"Yeah, fuck that!"

Ojeda shook her head and started up the curved base, rushing up the column.

Thomson called down, "It's almost here! What do we do?"

Ojeda made it around the transition hump and onto the platform, out of sight.

Asaaluk started up the column now.

Granger winced. "Where are you going?"

"If it's not those c-creatures in the elevator, we can use it to get back into the station—maybe straight up to the drill-truck and supply shipping docks at the base of the tube."

Granger nodded, catching on. "Yeah, yeah. Good idea. Then we could take the lifts there up the tube to the plug base."

Sidd wasn't sure that was smart, but they didn't have any better options.

The radiation from Jupiter punished the surface of Europa, so much that they couldn't keep an exposed base there. The plug base was a subsurface ring structure around the mouth of the bored out cylindrical shaft—or "tube"—from the surface, down to the facility they were in. The plug was a huge disc of shielding over this, its diameter such that it could cover the mouth and the base levels, concentrically connected around it.

Granger followed Asaaluk up, and Sidd felt a pang of something like betrayal pierce his fear and dread. He knew it was stupid to feel that way, but Granger hadn't even looked to him for agreement.

Sidd glanced at Biddle, who gripped his auto-rifle with a wild glare fixed above. Not great company.

Sidd followed the others up the column.

He came up around the path hump and onto the elevator platform. Ojeda was aiming her pistol at the sealed ring of metal where the elevator would open up upon docking, Granger just behind and to her side. Sidd crossed to them, seeing Thomson and Asaaluk half-cowering in shuddering anticipation near the channel for the path she'd come back up.

The freight elevator level display shimmered above the sealed ring in the center of the platform, counting down to the disc of freight elevator landing flush with where most of them were standing.

Sidd heard a light shuffling behind him and looked back. He could see Biddle's big eyes and the top of his head—plus the thick business end of his rifle—peeking up from around the surface of the path's hump. Wired but ready.

Sidd heard the freight elevator docking and locked his eyes back on the cylindrical door.

The hydraulic, metallic sounds were loud enough that none of them could hear each other shaking.

The light from Ojeda's hover drone reflected off the closed plasteel cylinder's glossy surface, so brightly that Sidd could make out silhouettes of those standing closest to it. He heard Biddle shuffling behind him, maybe inching closer for a good shot. But to hear him tell it—and from what they'd seen down there with their own eyes—they didn't have much chance anyway if the creatures came for them.

The docking sounds ceased and the cylinder around the elevator descended away, revealing—

Khondji, Vanlint's underling—and he was hurt bad.

There was bright, freshly spilt blood all over the elevator surface—pooling strangely over the puddles of slime and older blood from the Staysec team they'd seen before, almost like oil in water—from its edge to where he was crumpled onto the floor. He'd removed his science division smock and wrapped it tightly around his right arm—and it was soaked through with blood. He looked half-conscious.

Asaaluk gasped and crossed to him.

"Dr. Khondji!"

Thomson followed and without a word started assessing Khondji's wounds. He crouched and gingerly unwrapped the tourniquet the man had made of his smock.

Sidd caught a glimpse of the wound and a fresh arterial pulsing from out of it before Thomson wrapped it back up tight.

Khondji's right hand and forearm had been split clean in half lengthwise somehow, starting where his ring finger met the base of the middle and separating all the way to just before his elbow. As Thomson had pulled the smock apart, the radius and ulna had come apart as well—almost forming a narrow V coming off the mangled elbow, each ending in a different section of Khondji's hand.

Asaaluk's eyes grew wide, but then something changed in them. "Is there a first aid kit down here?"

"Yeah," Granger snapped, "—down on the pool deck."

He bolted without waiting to be asked, passing Biddle who'd finally made it up onto the platform with them. His gun was pointed at the ceiling for safety, but he was still geeked to high heaven.

In less than a minute, Granger was back with the medical kit. Asaaluk took it from him and she and Thomson went to work. They weren't surgeons, but knew enough about biology from their intensive schooling that they looked it.

Only a few minutes after that, Khondji's blood-drenched smock was tossed away and replaced with something like a transparent combination of tourniquet, cast, and sling. It even had intravenous injection catheter ports and AR blood pressure readouts and such hovering above it, once they'd finished.

There was also a small wound in Khondji's abdomen, but it didn't seem nearly as severe so they just cleaned and bandaged it after taking care of his mangled arm. Thomson used the IV ports on the special omni-tourniquet to administer a nano-synth blood pack, pain killers, and some kind of stimulant, Sidd assumed, because Khondji started groaning and mumbling almost immediately.

"Wh-where?"

Asaaluk watched Khondji's glowing AR vital signs, face forced to be neutral as she spoke. An attempt at bedside manner, Sidd figured. "You are on the moon pool deck. You were badly injured."

Khondji looked around through glossy eyes. "Losing...blood. Just pressed...first thing...I saw. My arm...."

"Yes, we have you stabilized."

Thomson said, "Relatively."

Asaaluk frowned at him.

Then Sidd heard that sound again—that trilling.

It was a fluttering warble that cut deeper into his twisting stomach with every note.

"They're comin'," he whispered.

They all went wide-eyed but stayed silent.

From the deformed gaps the creatures had made when forcing their way up into the elevator shaft, Sidd and the others could hear sounds of sliding and flapping along with the trilling.

Then louder.

Closer.

Sidd's mind raced—they needed a way out but there wasn't one.

Couldn't use the freight elevator they were in—those things would just climb down into it.

Thumping, slapping got louder from the shaft.

Couldn't use smaller elevators like the one they'd come down—no way to know if they would work with the trillers so close, then they'd be extra trapped.

More trilling.

Couldn't go up, couldn't go d—

It slammed into his mind, simultaneously amping him up and chilling his core with dread.

"The dive-suits."

They all looked at Granger like he was crazy, the others incredulous or confused.

"It's the only way—we go out through the moon pool, close it, climb to central—"

"You saw what we saw—central's full of those things," Ojeda whispered with him, eyes pointed upward, listening to the trillers descending.

"So we swim to one of the outer domes, or climb one of the fingercuffs."

"The what?"

Granger winced. "He means the evac bridge tunnels."

"And what about Khondji?" Ahmad asked.

Sidd scowled at her. "You patched him up, good as he can be. He don't need both arms if we help him along. There's no other way."

They all looked at him, then each other.

Flight it was.

Without further discussion, Granger started easing Khondji up to his feet with Asaaluk helping. Thomson had been calm enough and confident during the impromptu surgery they'd performed, but without that to focus on, he was awkward and skittish again. He couldn't help with hands, so he followed after them as they shuffled quickly toward one of the paragrav channels.

It was Sidd's plan, but he was still indecisive. He had no gun and couldn't fight the creatures like he would a drunken bar patron.

But in the confusion of the moment, he didn't feel right leaving it all to Ojeda and Biddle.

Ojeda made it easy, looking back with a steely gaze.

"Go—we got this...."

Sidd nodded and she returned it. He hurried toward one of the paragrav paths parallel to the others—

But he came around the hump too fast, throwing off his equilibrium and sending him into a rough tumble down onto the column pathway.

Sidd hauled himself up and went into as close to a sprint as a fresh limp would allow. He still beat them down, and started prepping dive suits.

Asaaluk, Granger, and Sidd helped Khondji into one, and the two men helped Asaaluk into her own.

Thomson was fumbling with a suit so Granger broke off to help him, as well.

Sidd looked down through the "glass-bottomed boat" of a deck between the moon pools and had to close his eyes and shake his head. The dark, swirling water out past the diffuse glow of the dome's exterior suggested many things—most he knew weren't there, but also things that could be. Those damn...trillers.

And trill they did.

Up on the elevator platform Ojeda and Biddle heard the haunting, piercing flutter of it, and it occurred to Ojeda that it was maybe like echo location or a means of communication between them—

Then they heard what had to be a few of the creatures dropping from the shaft interior wall and thumping down onto the elevator roof with sickening, heavy, wet slaps.

The light from the elevator went out entirely—and Ojeda's drone light flickered, almost cutting out.

"Shit."

She used her free hand to take out a chemlight from her jumpsuit, cracked it, shook it, and secured it back into its translucent pouch—

Just as the trillers started sliding and wriggling back in through a few of the openings the larger group of them had made when they climbed out and up.

Her drone's light faded out entirely and the unit dropped to the platform floor, clattering down uselessly and leaving the glow of her chemlight as the only source of luminosity.

In that glow that seemed to only barely cut through the inky darkness, what little she could see of the trillers' squirming, ever-changing bodies through their obscuring uncanny haze almost snapped something in her mind.

It was like their viscous and murky amorphous interiors could be almost solid and even bony under their translucent, stretched-skin-like outer surfaces—only to shift and become pulsing and shapeless again the next moment.

Ojeda screamed as she fired her shock pistol at one of the impossible-seeming creatures.

It let out something like a trilling shriek and retracted up into the opening.

Biddle fired his auto-rifle at what little was visible of the other monsters, also causing them to shrink up and away.

Down below, Sidd and Granger were unsealing the moon pool hatch while the others watched, all of them almost fully suited up and ready—as much as they could be, at least, to dive into an alien ocean that had so recently proven their worst primal fears about its possible predatory inhabitants to be true. Their helmets were still collapsed in storage compartments like rounded half donuts behind their heads.

Asaaluk and Thomson held Khondji upright, but all of them trembled and shuddered as the two techs worked.

As they finished, Sidd heard more gunshots and looked up at the platform. Other than a dim glow from what had to be a chemlight, all he saw were flashes when the guns fired.

"Dammit, they need to—Granger, get them into the water and climb toward one of the finger cuffs."

"What if we can't get inside?"

"I never worked on those but there's gotta be a way. But if you can't, the suits have rebreathers and they'll last for hours. Keep tryin' anywhere you can—better than this trapped rat shit, guaranteed!"

Granger grabbed Sidd's shoulder and squeezed.

"I'll see you soon. And don't forget your hat."

Sidd looked up and saw his lucky hat's bright orange bill. He nodded to Granger, then took it off, folded it, and tucked it in a zippered pouch on his dive suit's chest as the comms tech helped the others into the murky, ominous water.

Sidd grabbed two of the other dive suits and rushed back up the central column. As much as he'd hurried up to it, he had to force himself up around the paragrav transfer hump—and with good reason, he decided, when he caught his first half-glimpsed impressions of the things trying to climb down through the rifts they'd pried open.

On Glamis-3, he'd wanted to see what the creatures looked like, but was too scared to look when he'd had the chance.

Now, he'd already caught a brief peek at Europa's trilling monstrosities, and he'd seen all he ever wanted to.

Ojeda fired a couple more shots, causing a triller to retract some from the impacts, but not as much as they had at first. "Fuck! Charge is almost out—or these things are sapping it!"

Biddle fired at the one she couldn't hold back, but his gun chirped empty. He grabbed another compact drum magazine from a pack around his waist and swapped it out.

"Mine's got radiation shielding for surface fights—I think that stops their energy distortion bullshit!"

Sidd knew that Biddle must be right, and a chill rushed over him as he realized the trillers' proximity could shut off the dive suit systems if they weren't shielded.

Ojeda tried to fire one more time but her pistol just murmured and cut out.

"Shit!"

Sidd steeled himself and stepped around the rest of the hump to cross to Ojeda.

"Here, put this on!"

She looked at him, dazed from what she'd seen already.

Sidd locked eyes with her. "We have to go, mall cop."

The last part jogged her mind a bit and she cringed before shaking her head and nodding affirmative.

She let Sidd help her legs into the suit on the platform surface. Sidd took Ojeda's shock pistol out of her hand and tucked it under one arm, then they made short work of getting her secured up to her neck—he zipped her pistol into one of the suit's large chest pockets.

He closed his eyes and held his breath as he pressed an activation button for the suit's regulation systems and self-diagnostics—even this close to the creatures, it beeped and hummed up into auto-check status.

He exhaled and nodded, happy to know he hadn't damned the rest to suffocate in their suits, even if a triller never got close enough to touch them.

Then Sidd crossed to Biddle, who was still firing every time he saw even a hint of a triller's malformed, ever-changing extremity creeping down through an opening.

Sidd opened the other dive suit he had brought and spread it open on the floor near Biddle's boots.

Biddle tried to step into the leg holes, while still keeping his focus on the elevator ceiling and its pried gaps—

More thumps and trilling were heard, then more trillers started trying to squeeze back down onto the elevator platform.

Biddle kept firing as Sidd and Ojeda got the dive suit up around his waist. Just before they could secure it, Biddle reached down with a free hand and took out his last ammo drum.

"This is all of it, then I'm out—get in the fucking water!"

Sidd and Ojeda kept pulling the suit up to help him into it—

Biddle elbowed them both away and started firing again.

"The water's their turf! We'll need a head start to have a chance!"

Sidd and Ojeda's eyes met. He was right and they knew it.

Sidd said, "We'll leave the hatch open—but you say you're out and we can shut it after you remotely!"

"Fuck yeah, I will!"

Sidd hurried to the paragrav path.

Ojeda slapped Biddle's armored shoulder a couple times and he nodded in return. Then she followed Sidd and they both hauled ass down the column, sounds of gunfire rattling off behind them all the way.

Sidd saw Granger ahead and above—in that strange, disk of a wall at the end of the column as their floor optical illusion—he plunged himself into the open moon pool. Other vague shapes moved through the murky half-light Sidd could see through the transparent floor—the scientists, he hoped.

A glowing symbol faded up in Sidd's AR overlay that he remembered meant "sync" and cycled between that and a question mark. He pressed it with a haptic jab as he ran.

His helmet formed out of its storage compartment around his face and head, mostly solid and opaque except for a vertical, elliptical bubble panel of clear plasteel from temple to temple, lower lip to forehead. Ojeda activated hers too.

Once their helmets' nano-seams sealed and disappeared and the airflow started, Sidd and Ojeda's AR meshes synced with their suits'—and all the others, showing Asaaluk, Thomson, Khondji, and Granger as faintly luminous low-poly wire meshes that filled in their unclear forms he'd seen out in the water through the clear floor.

They were scrambling across the inverted dome's outer surface, the gloves, kneepads, and boots of their dive suits giving extra grip when in contact with any surface.

Sidd activated dive suit comms. "Show 'em how to hop, Granger."

–Hop? Never been outside in the drink—I don't even know how to do that....–

"Suits and dome got a kind of magnetic attraction system. Push off and up to get you glidin' through the water, jump jets in the packs kick in to take you farther, then instead of droppin' away, the dome pulls you toward it. Takes gettin' used to, but it's a lot faster than climbin' like that."

As he and Ojeda climbed into the moon pool, Sidd saw Granger stop, ready, and spring himself up and away, easily sailing past the others and through the water, then wave his arms like he was a bit panicked as he was drawn back to the dome and made contact.

-Yeah, much faster!-

Then, to the scientists Granger said, "-Okay, everybody—do what he said and the system kind of takes over for a few seconds."

Sidd and Ojeda readied themselves, boots hooked into the maintenance ring in the water and gloved hands gripping the edge of the moon pool opening.

Sidd looked at her and their eyes met through their helmet faceplates. She closed hers.

"I don't want to do this, Sidd...."

He grabbed her cushioned suit-covered forearm and forced a smile.

"Girl, me neither."

She opened her eyes and returned her own half-smile.

He nodded. "Okay, on three, right?"

She nodded.

"One...two...." Sidd said, bringing his body up and down in time with the words, and Ojeda following by suggestion.

Sidd took one last look up at Biddle's flashing gunshots and finished his count, "...Three!"

And they both plunged themselves into Europa's dark ocean.

NINE

Sidd had dived before, and far deeper, with suits that needed much more robust pressure mitigation—but he'd never felt so primally terrified as he did just then, looking into the gaping black maw of the ocean around and below the station. Gazing down into the stygian gloom of Europa's sea, he couldn't fight the feeling that the darkness would collapse around him, swallowing them all before the creatures had their chance.

So he focused on the dome and the others—and climbing away from all that maddening, inky blackness. At least open space had planets and stars.

Even verging on panic, Ojeda was a quick learner. Like Sidd, she'd dropped into the water and grabbed the maintenance ring around the moon pool exterior that their boots had just been supported by. But while he was clawing himself back from his moment of terror and vertigo, she did something like a pull-up, but kept going—flinging herself upwards in the water. The small jets in her suit's pack kicked on like Sidd had said and she glided up around the convex curvature of the moon pools' inverted dome exterior, toward the central structure. Then the magnetic attraction system brought her back into contact with the dome surface in a tight arc.

It took a second for her to gain purchase—the artificial traction system taking some getting used to—then she tucked into a crouch at her arms' greatest extension and sprung upward again.

Sidd did his own pull-up and fling motion and sailed up around the bottom third of the moon pool exterior. Coming around that far, he was able to see Granger and the others starting up the central dome's curve. As he came into contact with the surface, he went straight into another springing motion as Ojeda had and glided up after her.

Nearing contact again, Biddle's firing inside the dome caught Sidd's attention. He clawed onto the exterior surface with his gloved hands, then pressed his knees and boots to it, the method he'd been taught for stopping in place on the station exterior.

Sidd could see through the dome but Biddle's synced glowing AR wireframe helped distinguish him in the dark between gunfire flashes. The Staysec trooper was still on the platform. Sidd knew Biddle had to be on his last ammo drum and going down the central paragrav column was going to take some suppressing fire out in the open.

"Biddle—you've got to get to the pool!"

-I know, I know!-

Biddle started backing across the platform, toward a paragrav path as he kept up his firing on the peeking trillers.

Sidd looked up and saw Ojeda, Granger, and the others getting higher and farther away with their hops, and wanted to keep going himself.

Biddle backpedaled halfway around the transfer hump but stopped, continuing to shoot. Once he stopped firing, those things were going to get in, and Sidd's stomach twisted at the thought. But if Biddle ran out of ammo first, he was screwed.

"Biddle, go!"

Biddle turned to rush down the column—

But wobbled from a flash of disorientation and tripped over his own feet, tumbling around the rest of the hump into a heap on the column proper.

-Shit! Shit!-

Biddle hauled himself to his feet, but even over the comms, Sidd heard the trillers coming down out of the elevator ceiling and across the platform—slapping, sliding, tumbling, striding.

Biddle started running, gun forgotten and hanging by its sling.

Sidd watched him look back and scream—but the only light was from Biddle's chemlight and the faint glow of the dome's interior surface on the far side—revealing only the trillers' dim silhouettes that seemed to grow out of the column as they ambulated strangely around the transfer humps—

Then the creatures' strange energy fields killed the power on the paragrav surfaces of the column and Biddle dropped the rest of its height.

At the end of his thirty-foot fall, Sidd heard snapping, along with the heavy thump of it.

Biddle let out a dazed, tortured moan, then came to.

-I can't move! C-can't feel my body! Please, anybody—come back and get me!-

Sidd stared at the trillers' dim silhouettes, swelling and pulsing as they climbed down the central column in the dark. He could hear them making their wet, nasty sounds and warbling calls in-between Biddle's moans and sniveling.

"I can't, Biddle...."

-Please!-

Sidd looked up and saw that the others had stopped in place on the central dome exterior and were looking down at him and Biddle. It hit him then what he had to do, and he brought up the remote moon pool hatch controls in his AR overlay. But he hesitated before pressing the CLOSE AND LOCK command.

He looked back down and saw a haunting glimpse of a triller as it came into the glow of Biddle's half-obscured chemlight.

"I'm so sorry...."

Sidd pressed the floating command key and watched the dimly glowing, rounded-rectangle shape of the open moon pool getting smaller as its hatch closed.

Biddle screamed until something took away his ability with a strangling gurgle amid sizzling sounds.

Sidd stared at the area in the darkness where Biddle's chemlight had been visible, now obscured by his own mangled body, or the trillers' who were making awful sounds of some kind of biological consumption.

Sidd brought up his comms overlay and muted Biddle's channel with a trembling hand.

None of the others said a word as they continued up the central dome exterior. What could they say?

He knew he'd had no choice. The trillers were too fast, and from the sound of it, Biddle had been paralyzed by the fall. And by the time he had made it back, the creatures would have made it out anyway...but knowing all that didn't help.

Just like after Glamis-3, Sidd would torture himself by replaying the Staysec trooper's desperate cries for help as well as the sounds of this horrible death in his mind for the rest of his own life.

Which might not be too far into the future if he didn't stay focused, he realized, flinging himself up into the water.

One hop farther and he arced onto the central structure's convex curve. Another hop. Large sections of the corridors and chambers he passed were bathed in darkness. Sidd tried not to think about what that meant for their chances.

Sidd saw Ojeda catching up with the rest when Granger came over comms.

–Made it to a maintenance hatch into central, but we're locked out—none of my codes work!–

"Damn! Keep goin' to that fingercuff—"

Sidd heard sounds of moaning plasteel and metal from below. He put more into his push off and hopped even farther.

Thomson said, –What was that?–

"They're tryin' to get out through the pool—"

–No! They're going to get to us—they'll find us!–

"We just have to get inside first, Thomson."

–And then what will we do? Hope the rest that are all over the station will just let us sneak by?!-

"Shut up, Thomson—we don't need that shit right now!"

-He's right! Try to keep calm...,- Asaaluk agreed.

Granger reached the lower end of the maintenance tunnel. Each end had an air and pressure lock accessible from inside the central base structure where ever it linked up, and on that section's underside for emergency access.

-Locked out here, too! I'm going to try a physical hack....-

He hooked a carabiner-tipped line from his suit's waist area to one of many metal rings installed all over the exterior to secure himself. Then popped open a maintenance panel to the side of the airlock hatch and went to work trying to get it open.

Asaaluk and a reluctant Thomson helped Khondji hop up to the tunnel end exterior, then she noticed Granger's use of the securing harness and did the same. She hooked Khondji's clip to a ring and went to help Thomson with his.

Thomson swatted her hand away. -I'm not tethering myself to that thing, like a chunk of bait on a line!-

-Suit yourself!-

Sidd sailed past the sealed hatch into central and saw that Ojeda had stopped about twenty feet below the others, watching him. He eased his next arc some and came up to her.

She'd been crying.

With comms muted, he figured. Right then, she looked just like he felt. Frazzled. Desperate. Unsure. Terrified.

She linked them in a private comms channel.

-You had to do it, Sidd. He hesitated too much and lost his chance. And he told us to leave him....-

Sidd knew she was trying to convince herself as much as she was trying to comfort him, but he needed to hear someone else say it, so he wasn't complaining.

He grabbed her suit by the shoulder, squeezed, then nodded—

Sounds came from below again.

Sidd looked down to see bubbles sliding up the central dome's exterior from the moon pool dome.

Sidd keyed back to open comms. "I think they're almost out,

Granger...."

-I'm close to being done—Gah!-

Electricity flashed and glowed between his hands and Granger pulled them back, pumping them into fists a few times and shaking them out.

-Shit! Need more time....-

Sidd watched more bubbles sliding up and heard more sounds of plasteel moaning and being wrenched.

"We don't have a lotta time, man."

The creatures trilled again. That and the deep darkness around the station when he looked down made him avert his gaze upward again to stave off vertigo and panic.

First, he saw that Khondji seemed to have lost consciousness, swaying in the water anchored between the end of his carabiner line and the grips the other two scientists had on his suit.

Just hold on, Khondji, he thought.

Then he caught sight of a tiny blinking light in the distance. Above them and close to the central dome, near where it straightened out before meeting the ceiling of ice and stretching up to the plug.

Geeky Pete—the drone—whirring and self-correcting its orientation where they'd put it on pause earlier.

He heard more trilling, and louder. Groaning plasteel, bending to its limits.

"Wait—Granger, you had to be recordin' Vanlint's drone recon this mornin', right?"

-Yeah, why?- he asked, gingerly reengaging with his hot-wiring.

The moaning from below ceased and more bubbles slid up the domes. Then the trilling got louder. Clearer.

"Just get that fuckin' hatch open, man."

Sidd brought up a menu interface for his AR overlay. Cafeteria schedules. News. Games. Porn. VR training programs—there, Remote Training Modules. He brought those up and navigated to Geeky Pete's official call designation.

NO ACCESS—IN USE

"Godammit."

He entered his code for using the station on the moon pool deck, then cancelled the drone-sub's current operation.

Thomson squeaked. -Oh, god—I see them! They're hunting for us!-

Granger shushed him. -Shut it, Thomson. Whisper, or keep your mouth shut.-

Asaaluk shuddered. -Why? C-Can they hear us?-

Granger shook his helmeted head as he worked.

-No, noise-cancelling helmets—in and out. Probably carried over from their mil-tech prototypes.-

-Then why—?-

Sidd scoffed. -Because hearin' that bullshit ain't helpin' anybody right now.-

He couldn't look down. His imagination was working overtime as it was without Thomson's hysterics, filling his head with thousands of strangely blurry, amorphous monstrosities rising up from below.

Their trilling was bad enough.

He tried to crack Geeky Pete again.

NO ACCESS—UNIT MUST RETURN TO CHARGING STATION

Asaaluk's voice almost caught in her throat.

-T-Thomson's right, though—they seem to be trying to locate us.-

Sidd bypassed the automated commands trying to send the sub back to the moon pools. It took a few quick, fumbling tries but he remembered a maintenance code one of the techs had given him for working on Pete when they weren't available.

Then the personal operator code again.

ACCESS GRANTED

"Now we're cookin' with gas...."

Sidd used the drone maneuvering interface to bring up its saved data access vid viewer.

Asaaluk gasped and Sidd looked up, ready to scold—but she and Thomson were staring down at him and Ojeda—or near them.

Ojeda grabbed his shoulder.

He looked at her wild-eyed gaze and followed her line of sight—

Just as one of the creatures trilled from the dark, murky water, only thirty feet from them.

Damn, they move fast, Sidd thought.

Even gliding and tumbling along that close, the triller was so hard to see.

The unnatural vagueness of the thing's shape and uncanny blurring of its hyper-malleable flesh made it just a shifting charcoal gray silhouette against the deep black of the sea. There were brief instances where the blur almost cleared and he could see into the bulk of its churning form—glimpsed layered fusings of malformed pitted black bones, their textures resembling something between obsidian and half polished volcanic rock. They formed and grew together impossibly—sometimes stretching the creature's translucent sac-like exterior to its limits—only to be reabsorbed and re-fused somewhere else that suited its odd movement. Liquid to sludge to bone, constantly, and all just to serve its self-swallowing movement.

Who knew what else it could do with a body like that? Sidd tried not to think about it—which wasn't too hard because looking at it was hypnotic. Like a maddening otherness Sidd couldn't reconcile in his mind.

But it was very real and it was practically looking at them, if it had anything like optical receptors.

Sidd scrubbed the saved footage in the drone back to the alien whales, pressed play and then boosted the volume of the clip when the trillers first showed up.

Almost nothing. Barely audible.

"Granger! it's not—"

-You didn't patch the output to the externals—I got it, Sidd, just need a second....-

The creature slowed in the water and trilled again.

Asaaluk made a strangled peep of a sound and started trying to swim and pull herself up the outer surface of the maintenance tunnel—but her carabiner-tipped line stopped her.

She fumbled and tore at it, finally detaching herself—then hopped as they had all so recently learned to.

"Stop! What are you doing?!" Sidd called over comms.

Her comms feed picked up a murmuring of gibberish, something kicking on her flight instinct and shutting out rationality.

Sidd thought maybe just the fleeting glimpses of the creature's actual form through the blurring had broken something in her mind, as it almost had in his.

The triller shifted and eased to a stop in the water, then seemed to focus a portion of itself upward toward the young woman. It trilled again, with a shifting tone.

Asaaluk arced up onto the dome, connecting with hollow thuds where her hands and knees met it, then propelled herself up again—

The triller bolted up toward her, its chaotic form spilling and clawing through itself as it was propelled by the strange motions.

Thomson gasped. -No! Stop moving!-

Granger stopped hard-wiring and switched to his AR overlay, quickly accessing Geeky Pete and routing the onboard audio to external speakers.

He said, -That's got it—you've got to stop making noise, Asaaluk! Go limp!-

-I c-can't!-

Asaaluk kept arcing upward and waved her arms like she wanted to stop, but the automated suit thrusters and mag system wouldn't allow it.

Ojeda clawed at Sidd's arm unconsciously, her breath sharp as well.

Sidd knew nothing could stop Asaaluk's movement in time—nothing but the triller, now beelining toward the sound of her thrusters—

It reached the young scientist with little effort, catching her just as the magnetic link was arcing her back toward the central dome exterior.

Asaaluk screamed as the creature's writhing body engulfed and obscured her from normal sight. Her suit's glowing wireframe was still visible, and Sidd couldn't look away as the triller started taking her apart.

Her cries of terror and pain were mixed with sounds of ripping and that strange sizzling—juxtaposed with an accidental surreality in how the wireframe tried to reconcile her suit being torn apart. The glitching was almost beautiful as the suit was stretched, torn, and unfurled.

Then her helmet must have come apart from the way the wireframe's head bent and fluttered, and her already gurgling cries became choked and muffled as water poured into her mouth. She started drowning as she was being taken apart.

Sidd could only hope there was some mercy in that, but it didn't sound like it.

He caught movement in his peripheral vision and saw the other trillers propelling themselves in the direction of Geeky Pete. Then the one above them followed, whatever was left of Asaluuk's body and suit going with it.

The broken and bent wireframe rotated, jerked, and twisted more as the monstrous thing's strange movement continued to contort and disfigure the young woman's body now inside its own ever-changing bulk. And whatever that sizzling sound was from seemed to be breaking it down too, parts of the wireframe disappearing from the whole as the sensors that projected them disintegrated—or were maybe digested.

Sidd felt sick from watching it all, and the fear and dread that came with thinking about it happening to him.

"Granger...."

–I know,– he said, already back to focusing on his wiring.

Thomson let out a breath that he must have been holding in.

–We are going to die...like her and all the others.–

Sidd couldn't argue so he didn't say anything at all. He just watched the vague forms of the trillers shifting and churning as they examined Geeky Pete—before destroying the drone and silencing the playback of their own warbling calls.

With the drone gone, the creatures started trilling again.

Then they contracted and pulsed through their own bodies as they swam and seemed to search for something—anything else to kill and consume. Whatever had made them what they were—natural evolution or something far stranger—they didn't seem to care about anything else.

Sidd shuddered in his suit and felt like he might lose control of his bowels or bladder. Maybe both.

-Got it!- Granger said and pulled his hands away from the guts of the panel as they flashed and glowed again—

But this time the lock's hatch opened, water rushing into it from the angle that it was oriented at.

Granger unhooked his carabiner and Khondji's, pulling the listless scientist along with Thomson's help as they swam and climbed up into the lock chamber.

Sidd patted Ojeda's helmet and she nodded. They both hopped up to the hatch opening on the underside of the maintenance tunnel and swam up into it.

TEN

The lock system's hatch closed and sealed below them, then started draining the water out of the chamber from above. Sidd let himself drift to the bottom, his heavy boots contacting the angled floor.

A canted slice of an air pocket started forming under the highest part of the chamber ceiling, growing quickly as the sea water drained from the walls and floor. Soon, there was just a slanted puddle around their feet, as they were near the lowest spot.

Thomson crumpled to the wet plasteel floor, just up from them and let out something between a pained sob and a cough.

Granger hooked Khondji's carabiner to a ring on the chamber wall and draped him in such a way that he wouldn't collapse, then turned his attention to the hatch between the tunnel and the central dome's exterior hatch to which it was docked against. He keyed some commands into a panel—then slammed the bottom of a gloved fist against it.

-Shit—locked out here too!-

Sidd checked his exterior air sensors, then popped his helmet.

The pieces came apart and tucked themselves down into the thick collar. He stepped down the incline to stand by Granger and put a hand on his left shoulder.

"We'll just go up the fingercuff...."

Granger took in a deep breath, then let it out in a shuddering sigh. He popped his helmet too and they locked eyes. Granger put his right hand on Sidd's forearm and squeezed, then patted it and nodded. Sidd felt a surge of connection between them, but had learned not to get his hopes up.

Thomson laughed mirthlessly. -Yes, let's just go up the fingercuff–I feel totally at ease under the guidance of this bumbling, provincial vehicle tech!-

Sidd gave Thomson a side-eyed look and let go of Granger's shoulder as he turned toward the verbally pugnacious scientist on the floor—

Ojeda beat him to it, hauling Thomson up to his feet and slamming him against the chamber wall.

-That vehicle tech just saved all of us! What were you going to do...cry on the fucking monsters?! He got us out of there!-

-And got the security soldier and Asaaluk killed in the process!-

Granger scoffed. "That was not his fault!"

Thomson laughed again. -I'm not entirely sure you understand what the word 'fault' means, then!-

Ojeda popped her helmet.

Sidd said, "Well, if you'd like t'go back out in the water, I'm sure those triller things would love to discuss matters of personal responsibility and causality with you...."

Thomson looked at Sidd and feigned amazement, then tried to find his helmet's open command key.

-I hope you aren't too fatigued from tripling your usual syllable count on that sentence, Mister Priddy.-

"I'm just fine, asshole."

"Let me help you with that, Thomson...." Ojeda said, then keyed his helmet open.

As it collapsed into Thomson's collar, Ojeda spit in his face.

"Go fuck yourself."

Thomson shook his head. "Idiots and barbarians—you people are vile refuse."

Khondji moaned where he was hanging.

Sidd laughed. "And you're a fuckin' delicate cockwomble."

Khondji moaned again and they all looked at him.

Granger crossed back and checked the vitals shimmering over the special tourniquet on Khondji's arm, squinting at them.

Thomson shrugged and squirmed out of Ojeda's grip to join Granger, wiping her spit and his own tears away on the thick fabric of his dive suit's arm.

"You don't know what you're looking at. Step aside."

Granger gave them space.

Thomson cringed and frowned at the hovering AR readouts.

"Dr. Khondji will die if we don't get him to a fully functional medlab."

"No arguments on that. But we also definitely need to keep moving," Sidd said as he hiked a few steps up to the maintenance tunnel hatch. He checked the panel next to it. "Structural integrity—check. Air—check. Tunnel inclination angle—twenty-seven degrees. Okay, I didn't get a good look at the tunnel before we made it into the lock, so cross your fingers, y'all...."

He keyed the large hatch open and it broke apart, the smaller sections retracting into storage channels.

The maintenance tunnel's long cylindrical structure foreshortened away and up into the distance, dark but empty—at least as far as Sidd could see. The water swirling around outside its upper half's clear plasteel structure caused ever-shifting shadows to dance around its interior. But it was long enough that the inky murk was impenetrable as it stretched closer to the looming inverted dome that was their destination.

Sidd produced his orange camo CAT hat from his suit's chest pocket, shaped it a bit and put it back on.

Granger chuckled and shook his head.

"For luck?"

Sidd looked back at him. "Always."

"Let's hope that counts for all of us...."

Ojeda looked up into the darkness on the far side of the tunnel. "Amen to that."

Granger crossed back to Khondji and hooked an arm under his back, draping the half-conscious man's unhurt arm across his own shoulders. He unhooked the carabiner from Khondji's suit and helped him up the inclined floor toward the tunnel proper.

Sidd shook his head as Thomson put his hand against Khondji's back, as if it would somehow help him along. At least he seemed to be keeping an eye on the AR vitals readout, which actually could be helpful.

Sidd turned and started up the inclined tunnel while the rest followed.

Similar to the paragrav column back in the moon pool dome, the center of the twenty-foot wide maintenance tunnel's walkway had special tracks for hauling equipment, but there was no paragrav paneling installed under the flanking walkways. Just rubberized ridges for traction. They made it about one-third of the way up the tunnel and Sidd could make out the hatch on the far side. It seemed clear the rest of the way.

Ojeda said, "Is that one of the science domes?"

Sidd shook his head. "Nah, Air Plant-Three."

"How can you tell?"

Sidd pointed.

"You see those dark, kinda...beveled circles near the bottom?"

"Yeah."

"Sea water intakes for the electrolysis systems."

Ojeda frowned. "Okay, that makes sense. But how do you know it's AP-Three?"

"He's got wayfinder up in his overlay," Granger said behind them.

"You got me."

Ojeda frowned. "Wayfinder?"

"It's an app they give us drivers and maintenance techs since we don't have overlay guidance signs outside of the station. I'm usin' the personal app. Drill-trucks have it built in, for navigatin'.

How else would we get to the Lake station, right?"

"I thought there was a subsurface tram from the Plug."

Sidd chuckled. "The tram's for amateurs."

In-between low moans, Khondji mumbled something.

Granger stopped. "What's that?"

Khondji forced out, "R'ceiving...trans...mission...."

Sidd judged them to be almost halfway up the tunnel and nodded.

"Let's hear what we can hear."

The scientist tried to sit and Granger helped him down to the slanted floor. Then he brought his portable comms interface from his personal menu and synced all of their overlays to Khondji's.

A distorted vid feed wavered and glitched into view in the periphery of their overlays. Sidd selected it with a finger jab in the air and it centered before him like a hovering, caseless monitor screen.

It was hard to make out, but oddly familiar.

Fixed view of something moving through darkness, beams of light burning ahead. Strange shapes like ominous, abstract statues looming in silhouette. Fleshy, but rusted-looking structure surfaces where the lights exposed it, sprouting fields of swaying bulb-covered—

The ancient alien machines they'd seen that morning through Geeky Pete's camera eyes. But if GP was just destroyed and the other drones were docked above their sealed moon pools...?

Sidd narrowed his eyes. "Khondji, what are we looking at?"

"It's...Hitomi."

"Vanlint?"

"Yes. She took...personal explorer sub...to anomalous...structures."

Hearing that, Granger adjusted something and the feed got clearer as a distorted voice could be heard.

–...–scinating. But I need to know what's ...–ppening, Khondji. Please ...–spond.–

Ojeda's eyes were glued to her overlay. "This is what you found? That's incredible...."

Thomson sniffed. "It truly is. It could change our whole view of the solar system, just as a starting point. Nothing like this has ever been found so close to Earth. We would have to survive this, though, for that to happen."

"What do you mean, so close to Earth? Have we found other things like this?"

Thomson smirked, mostly to himself. "I may have said too much."

Ojeda said, "Yeah, seems that way."

Khondji shook his head. "He knows...nothing. Just...rumors. Don't listen...to him."

"Either way, he ain't wrong about nothin' comin' of it if we can't get out of here alive."

Sidd tried to activate comms through the feed connection. No good. "Granger, can you connect me?"

Granger nodded and fiddled. Then he pointed at Sidd, a silent gesture to start.

"Hello, Dr. Vanlint."

–Who ...–this?–

"Sidd Priddy, ma'am. I'm here with Khondji but he's hurt real bad. The station has been...infested. Overtaken by the creatures we saw this mornin'—the ones that chased the whales away."

–You're cut...–ng out. Khondji's hurt and cr...–ures have infested the sta...–on?–

"Yes, they followed the drone, came in through moon pools, and just started...slaughtering people."

–I see.... Yes, they seemed quite agr...–sive.–

Ojeda scoffed. "Aggressive would be a safe description!"

Thomson glared at her. "Show Doctor Vanlint some respect!"

"Oh, I'm sorry—does she fascinate you? Is she extra super smart and pretty? Do you want to hold hands with her and have a sneering competition?!"

Sidd looked up at the layered, padded plasteel arches that partially overlapped each other to create the flexibility of the maintenance tunnel at different angles. When Thomson and Ojeda's voices got loud, the arches above them vibrated in time with the syllables.

"Maybe you all should calm down a bit...."

But Ojeda wasn't done. "Yes, let's find a specimen of inferior intellect and see who can give them the sharpest uninterested down the nose glare!"

Sidd heard distant trilling.

Thomson raised his eyebrows. "We're too intellectual or educated? Is that your issue? I'm not surprised, though, coming from a—what did Granger call you? A mall cop? But you're not even competent enough to protect anyone, are you? Maybe you'd be a more capable inventory clerk!"

"You sniveling prick!"

Ojeda moved toward Thomson with clenched fists—then stopped when she heard—

More trilling. Louder. Closer.

Vanlint said, -Are the pred...-ry creatures making th...-oises? Maybe if y—-

But the signal cut out.

Then Sidd saw them—almost-black forms, their ever-shifting bone-jumble internal structures, silhouetted now by the glow of the central dome above and behind them in stark contrast, with their exterior sacs, and whatever fluids were encased in them, more translucent.

Three trillers approached the tunnel from above. Then, as they reached it they started focusing their calls, examining its structure.

One of the creatures trilled loudly.

Sidd felt it vibrate in his bones, and pictured it seeing them as rough structures formed from echo reflection speed. If they could see any other way, he doubted they did it very well.

The triller closest to the tunnel ceiling produced a new blobby appendage at will, of self-replicating black bone in viscous muck, stretching its skin sac taut in that area of its form as it grew.

It slid the growth across the plasteel surface above them, causing a barely audible squeaking sound.

Then it trilled to the others, as far as Sidd could tell, and they all glommed onto the tunnel's upper exterior. Sidd heard what sounded like...sizzling?

Granger whispered, "What are they doing?"

Sidd decided that whether or not they could see, they seemed to already know he and the others were there. He looked down at the floor and took the chance that the divesuits' shielding extended to their shoulder lights, and activated his.

The illumination popped up from behind both of his shoulders on articulated arms, overlapping conical beams pointed down at the angled tunnel floor where he was looking. The lights pulsed and flickered like they would shut off, but kept lighting up sporadically.

He looked back up, the lights tracking with his head and giving intermittent flashes of the trillers pressing strange organs Sidd hadn't seen yet against the plasteel. The pumping nodule covered flesh making contact with the tunnel surface was seeping out some bubbling fluid—

And eating away at the clear plasteel.

"Oh shit—let's go!"

Sidd hooked an arm under Khondji and hauled him up with a wide-eyed Granger's help. They hurried up the inclined tunnel as fast as they could.

Sidd looked back as they hiked, his shoulder lights pulsing and flashing back toward Thomson and Ojeda.

Thomson was frozen in place, staring up at the barely visible creature closest to him.

Ojeda grabbed him and tried to pull him along—but he broke free from her grasp, transfixed on the creatures above.

"Come on, shithead!"

The creatures' fluids began seeping down from the first of the openings they were making—then pouring and burning into the tunnel floor. Ate it away like it was nothing.

It reminded Sidd of one time he was working a loading dock and some idiot dropped a keg of acetone off of their elevated forklift pallet. It split and sprayed out onto a big stack of the old kind of packing foam they'd had lying around that was illegal now. Wherever it touched—gone in seconds.

The sight was enough to finally get Thomson snapped back to

reality. Ojeda grabbed his arm and this time he didn't fight, following her up the angled tunnel floor.

There was a sizzling and sucking sound—and the waters of Europa's sea erupted up from the holes made from the trillers' fluids. Spilling. Gushing. Then rushing down the inclined surface to pool against the canted sealed hatch of the airlock they had left just moments before.

Then the water started rising.

"Close your helmets!" Sidd yelled before grasping Khondji's arm again and continuing to carry him with Granger's help. The others followed their lead up the tunnel, closing their helmets as Sidd had directed. He tucked his hat away again and closed his own.

They were over two-thirds up the tunnel when the trillers broke all the way through, dropping down with squishing slaps onto the angled floor—

As more of Europa's sea water followed them in—roaring and splashing down into the tunnel as it rushed to meet the rising water from the acid burned openings.

In only seconds, the tunnel was halfway full, and the structure groaned from the awkward weight of it.

Sidd and Granger, with Khondji between them reached the upper airlock hatch and Sidd pressed it to cycle—the tunnel breach had locked them out.

"Granger."

"I know, I know."

They set Khondji down and Granger popped open the maintenance panel.

Sidd turned back and looked down.

All he could see other than Ojeda and Thomson's glowing link wireframes were silhouettes of the trillers and deep dark of the rising water—with flickering pulses that lit up the tunnel but didn't burn that far down into it.

In the quick glimpses, it looked like the trillers had trouble moving and ambulating outside of the water. Or had to get used to the transition. They flopped around, whipping chaotically forming, tentacular limbs with malformed digits, trying to gain purchase.

Then he caught sight of one of them combining the amorphous limb growths with sharp hooks or talons formed from their layering black bone, whatever that really was.

But it worked, and that creature trilled up the tunnel as it started climbing from talon hold to talon hold.

Sidd was transfixed, his stomach knotting as images of what those creatures could do to him with their will-controlled black bone hooks, blades, and who knew what else.

Another triller tried something similar with its form, but flung itself up onto the curved ceiling of the tunnel, using its hooked appendages to climb the layered plasteel plates above. It was a sac of pus, bones, and organs performing a bad impression of a headless chimpanzee, only gigantic by comparison and letting out a warbling trill between each swing from hold to hold.

The farther the trillers made it up the tunnel and closer they got, the more Sidd's shoulder lights flickered—and the less he could see them.

Sidd had never wanted a weapon in his trembling hands so badly before in his life.

"Mate...?"

"Almost got it, Dusty!"

The ceiling climbing creature was faster, catching up with Thomson and Ojeda, about thirty feet down the incline from Sidd and the others.

It whipped a thin black tendril down through one of Thomson's legs and severed it—so cleanly that he moved to take another running step with a lower leg that wasn't there. He toppled as his body kept going and collapsed, blood spurting from the fresh wound.

The tunnel moaned from the water filling it, drowning out most of his screams as he clutched at his knee and the spasming remnants of his cleaved lower leg.

Ojeda was panicked enough that she made it another fifteen or so feet before looking back and by the flickering lights saw that Thomson was down. She spun, fumbling with her chest pocket until she pulled out her glitching shock pistol—

Just as the creature who had hobbled Thomson dropped down near him, almost obscuring him from Ojeda's view.

She tried to fire her pistol but it just made a buzzing sound.

The triller rose from the slanted floor and loomed as it flapped and slurched down toward him.

Sidd scanned his shoulder lights back and forth down the tunnel, with tight swiveling head movements, trying to keep the other two creatures in sight—but the trillers' approach weakened and distorted the lights more and more.

Granger exhaled sharply. "Got it!"

The hatch to the upper airlock hissed as it broke apart and Granger started helping Khondji up into its chamber.

The tunnel shuddered as the sea water filled over three quarters of its length, something it was not designed for.

Ojeda tried her gun and again it pulsed—then fired, sending a visible bolt down into the triller near Thomson—

The creature pulsed and seized up—but it was close enough to Thomson that this caused it to collapse down onto him, enveloping all but his still intact leg as it flopped around him and rolled down into the rising water.

"No!" Ojeda screamed.

Then Sidd caught a glimpse of something above Ojeda—

A thicker tendril from one of the other trillers flapped down and around Ojeda's pistol arm—

It burned through her suit with the acid, and with no obvious effort pulled her arm off at the shoulder.

"Ojeda!" Sidd yelled stretching an arm in her direction, out of instinct—

But Ojeda was already bleeding too much—the wound only partially cauterized—and when she tried to turn back up the incline, she slipped on her own lifeblood and tumbled backwards, plunging into the water before the creatures could renew their attack.

The tunnel groaned again and part of its ceiling buckled, opening a new rift that added a fresh surge to the rising water.

Granger grabbed Sidd's suit by the collar.

"Dusty, come on!"

Sidd looked up at Granger, then back down the tunnel—

His lights glinted across two trillers climbing the tunnel ceiling toward them.

"Shit!" Sidd cried then hauled himself up into the airlock chamber with Granger's help.

Granger activated the hatch and it closed as the water was less than ten feet below them, and rising with a quickness.

The hatch sealed as Granger and Sidd breathed heavily in their slumped positions against the chamber floor. Khondji moaned and mumbled to himself. With the tunnel still groaning and shifting, it struck Sidd as almost comical, like the gravely injured scientist and the damaged structure were competing for attention.

From his spot on the canted, shuddering floor, Granger activated his overlay and accessed the hatch that would get them into Air Plant-Three.

Still breathing heavily, Granger said, "Fan...tastic...."

"What?"

Granger linked their personal overlays. Sidd saw an open message from Vanlint that was just an alphanumeric code, about ten digits long.

Then he saw in a faintly glowing notification area of his peripheral vision in his overlay that he'd received the same message.

"She must have...sent it...while we were talking. Or right after. Looks like it was supposed to be for just Khondji...but the link sent it to all of us."

Sidd looked up at the dome's hatch. "Must have. That'll get us in?"

"It should—"

Something slapped hard against a porthole window on the side hatch and they flinched.

Sidd stood up and looked.

It was Ojeda, her helmet pressed up against the window—held in place by one of the trillers. From the look in her eyes, she had lost a lot of blood, but she was still able to lock eyes with Sidd.

A deep chill ran through him from the nightmarish sight of his dying friend desperately glaring at him. Then he heard a sound that made him shudder too.

Sizzling.

Ojeda tried to look behind her with wild eyes but couldn't move.

She screamed as the triller's acid ate through the back of her helmet. Water poured in and she started sputtering and choking—but then the acid oozing from the triller's body reached the back of her head. She tried to scream but it became more like an animal moaning as the acid ate into her skull and brain from the back.

Granger closed his eyes tight and swallowed. "Sidd, don't watch!"

But he couldn't look away.

The triller pumped its body against the back of Ojeda's head and body almost obscenely as it used its fluids to eat away at her. Her eyes still rolled around, sightless but moving when the acid reached the back of her face. Then one was burned away, and the other.

A sorrowful howl caught in Sidd's chest and came out strangled and wheezing.

Then the creature's acid made short work of Ojeda's helmet faceplate—

And the creature pulled away enough that water started gushing in—through where their friend's head had just been.

In seconds, it was up to Sidd's knees and Granger and Khondji's ankles, a bit above him.

Granger hurried to input Vanlint's code. The hatch into Air-Plant-Three broke apart and opened onto near darkness and the low thrumming of its machinery.

He picked up Khondji as best he could on his own.

"Sidd...?"

Sidd didn't know how deliberate it had been on the creature's part, but he'd never witnessed something that brutal and cruel.

He had never felt hate for the creatures on Glamis-Three, awful and merciless as they were.

But he sure did hate these goddamn trillers.

Then the one that had killed Ojeda started squirming its way in through the porthole, somehow able to make its form narrow enough, like flowing slime or something similar. Sidd had seen octopuses on Earth forcing themselves through tight holes on fishing ships in a similar way—

Granger grabbed Sidd and he came to his senses, turning and helping his friend carry Khondji's half-conscious body up into the hatch and closing it.

Sidd heard trilling, along with shuddering moans of plasteel and turned back to look out through the clear plasteel hatch—just as the tunnel buckled and detached, taking the airlock and creature with it. Out in the dark sea water between AP-3 and Central, the glitching and distorting AR wireframes of Thomson and Ojeda's suits disintegrated in those creatures' weird guts.

He watched the glowing skeletal polygon figures disappear for one more long moment, then deactivated his wireframe sync setting. They mercifully blinked out entirely in his overlay.

And all he saw was black water.

ELEVEN

Khondji's helmet-muffled moans could be heard among the Air Plant's pumping, thrumming machine sounds, pulling Sidd back into the moment. They had taken on a chilling oddness that made him fear the worst for the scientist's condition and chances.

He peered down the corridor, lights blinking from piston-like electrolysis machinery that flanked it and a faint glow from the dome's exterior surface illumination, their only sources of faint visibility.

Granger opened his helmet. "We aren't going to make it."

Sidd popped his own. "What?"

"Even if we get into Central...those things are probably everywhere at this point. And I'd be surprised if there are any doctors left who can help him."

Sidd looked at Khondji. "They've got med-pods that can fix him up without help. Robots and shit like that."

"If we live long enough to find one."

Out of habit, Sidd took out his lucky hat, flapped it back into shape, and nestled it onto his sweat-covered brow.

Granger let out an incredulous, short breath.

"Is your hat really important right now, Dusty?"

"About as much as anything else, I guess."

Granger looked like he might cry, then laughed mirthlessly as he shook his head.

"We're fucked."

"So, your plan is to just, what...sit here an' be fucked?"

Granger stared down into the grated metal floor next to Khond-ji and slumped his shoulders. Terrified. Exhausted. And something else.

Defeated.

Sidd couldn't help feeling all those same things, if he was being honest with himself. He'd felt them before, too, on Glamis-Three.

But he hadn't died there.

Why?

Why was he still alive?

Because he was smarter than he seemed—and twice as stubborn.

And how did he get through it? He'd gathered what he needed to stay alive, then set out toward salvation. Only stopping when his body gave out. In the absence of weapons, he had fought hard, in his own way, to survive.

Sidd had never been clear on what he believed, cosmically or religiously or whatever—but no matter what was or wasn't out there, the urge that drove him to survive had taken him just far enough to be saved.

Deep-seated "reptile brain" survival instincts or Divine Providence...Sidd believed human beings, like most other animals, had evolved to be fighters, for better or worse. Figuratively. Literally. Fight for food, water, breath.

Breath.

Sidd felt a spark of possibility. "The drill-trucks."

Granger looked up, puzzled.

"We grab extra air tubes for a drill-truck and just fuckin' drive it out into the ice shell. If we're quick an' quiet, they'd prob'ly never come after us. And drill tunnels would collapse after us pretty quick, warmin' up from the heated air the drillin' produces. Then we'd be in a little movin' island fortress, monster-fuckin'-free."

Granger's eyes darted around, calculating.

"But, how long do the air tubes last?"

"A couple days, each. It's like...concentrated and tweaked a bit for longer duration. Smells and tastes weird and your lungs tingle some after a while, but you can breathe it. We grab some rations. The trucks have mini-electrolysis machines built in, always producin' drinkable water into little reserve tanks from the ice they melt away.

"We go out and camp in the ice, wait a few days. Cabin fever is our biggest challenge. A little claustrophobia. Maybe the goddamned trillers get bored and swim back down to their whatever-it-is. Even if they don't, we wait a while then drill up to the plug base and you use the gear there to call in the cavalry."

Granger thought a bit more.

Sidd forced a smile. "Hey, we gotta get to those islands, right? Sailin' around...fishin'...dumb Tiki drinks."

Granger forced his own half-smile in return.

"Okay. Let's do it."

Sidd nodded and Granger returned it.

They tried to help Khondji to his feet, but he was limp. He moaned, gibbering almost inaudibly.

"Should we pop his helmet?"

Sidd shook his head. "Nah, the suit's air is probably better for him right now than all this wet humid shit."

Starting along, he would gain footing every few steps, so they carried him like that as they traversed the dark rows of pumping machinery.

Small, glowing lights on the machines were the only things aiding Sidd's depth perception, as their more jumbled silhouettes went through different motions in the dark. Even if the trillers couldn't see much, he didn't want to chance turning his shoulder lights back on and giving away their position.

After several wrong turns and a couple dead ends, Sidd led

them to the air tube distribution storage racks.

They eased Khondji onto the floor and crossed to a set of hooks on the wall next to a set of tube racks that held carrier packs.

The drill-truck bays up on the docking level had automated forklift-carried shipments of air tubes, but the packs were there for drivers and techs who didn't have time to wait for them.

The air tubes were about eight inches in diameter and a few feet long, and there were two and three slot packs. Sidd figured if they needed more than four between them—about a week's worth—they probably didn't have much of a shot anyway. He handed Granger a two-slot pack and helped him sling it over his dive suit, then put one on and Granger returned the favor. Sidd loaded Granger's two tubes then turned around.

Khondji started moaning louder and more strangely as Granger was loading Sidd's first tube. Then he started shaking where he sat on the floor.

Sidd whispered, "Shit, don't die on us, man...."

Granger loaded the second air tube. "We've got to get him to a med-pod."

"Next stop, med-pod. Sure thing. And maybe we should pop his helmet. I don't know much about medical shit."

"Right, okay...."

Granger stepped over to Khondji, hooked an arm under his, and helped him up. Then he activated his helmet collapse function.

The helmet broke apart, revealing—

The upper half of Khondji's head was still Khondji—but everything under his wide, bulging eyes—and unevenly bisecting his head crosswise—was translucently gelatinous with the bones like pitted black rock. Teeth, jaw, skull, spine—then, with the helmet opened, those parts started moving on their own.

In a flash of understanding and utter terrified revulsion, Sidd saw that Khondji's eyes and most of his brain were still him—but everything else was triller. Complete with a shifty blur when he tried to look below the scientist's eyes.

Granger tried to speak—

The triller part of Khondji bulged in the dive suit, then the parts that had been bone and jaw jutted out instantly, piercing Granger's face near his left cheekbone like a long organic icepick.

It pulled its sharp appendage back out, causing blood to spurt onto Khondji's wild, still-human upper face and head. The tortured remnants of the man's consciousness came through in his mad eyes.

Granger tried to push the thing away from him—but it bulged and tore at the suit until the seams burst and it was only half intact.

Then it wrapped its form around Granger, its movements a mockery of the roughly human form the shredded suit still tried to maintain.

It took every ounce of courage Sidd still had to step forward and try to pull Granger free—the triller under Khondji's brain struck out, whipping a slicing tendril toward Sidd.

He ducked, still trying to grab Granger's arm—

The triller wrapped its form tighter around Granger and took him to the ground, sending a spike of black bone out into Sidd's shin, dropping him to the grated floor.

"Gah!"

Granger meant more to Sidd than anything else on the station—so even from his side on the floor, he tried again, getting both of his arms between his friend and the creature—

It shot out a thin spike, grazing against the side of Sidd's skull, searing a pencil-thick channel of flesh and skull out of his head right above the temple and piercing the band of his lucky orange hat before sucking back into the monstrous thing—

Then another of its spines went through his shoulder on the same side.

Sidd cried out but tried to fight it.

Then the thing bulged from just under Khondji's upper head that was being consumed with each moment, opening some undulating flaps in what had been the man's face—

And it started trilling.

Then another returned its call.

Sidd couldn't tell how far away the other was, but he finally had confirmation of his fear that there was at least one proper triller in the AirPlant dome with them.

Its first reply trill was muffled from distance and the pumping machines.

Its second was louder, clearer—and way closer than he could handle. Either there was more than one big one in AP-Three, or they had already learned to move with a deeply frightening quickness out of the water.

Sidd's instincts took over and he transferred all of his effort to getting free from Granger and the thing that was now almost all the way out of Khondji.

The other triller called again, maybe fifty feet away down one of the corridors and Sidd flailed and broke free.

Granger reached for him. "Dusty!"

"I c-can't...."

He turned and ran harder than he ever had, hoping he'd picked the right direction—and that the pulsing, thrumming machine's muddled the sounds of his escape.

TWELVE

Sidd had chosen roughly the correct direction, if he wanted back into Central. He did and he didn't, but now he had no choice. His mind screamed at him to go back but his instincts kept him going farther away.

YOU SHOULD HAVE FOUGHT HARDER!
But I had no choice....

He slowed to a creep—which took real effort because his heart was thumping hard in his chest and he felt a little dizzy—as he approached the hatch into Central and peered into a porthole window in its surface. It was dimly lit from glowing emergency strips flanking the corridor walkway.

YOU LEFT GRANGER!
We'd both be dead now if I hadn't....

Sidd took a chance and activated the hatch. It wasn't quiet but could've been louder. Didn't hear any trilling, at least.

YOU LET HIM DIE!
I had no choice....

He entered the corridor and crept down it, coming to a T intersection. Looked left and right. More dark corridors with glow strips running along their gentle curves.

THOSE THINGS ARE FUCKING KILLING HIM!
I had no choice. I have to keep moving.
I have to survive.

Straight ahead there was a door made of clear plasteel.

Inside, glitching emergency lights were illuminating the large rec room—the same one in which he and Granger had been playing Warp Pong in earlier, only he was viewing it from the other side of where they'd left from, so recently and so long ago.

Sidd tried the door panel with a shaking hand and it worked, sliding away into the wall.

As he slipped through the rec room, he listened for signs of danger, but his mind drifted as he passed the ping-pong table.

The paddles were still resting there, one propped at an angle against a ball.

They'd had such good times there—

Trilling.

Sidd froze in place, panic gripping him. His hands shook and insides shuddered as he looked around for any salvation. What he wouldn't have given for a flamethrower unit or an auto-rifle right about then. His eyes rested on the ping-pong table—he could just fit into the negative space under its curved base like a snug little cave. He slipped his tube carrier pack off and tucked himself under the table, pulling the pack in behind him.

He remembered his bright orange hat and pulled it off, tucking it back into his chest pocket.

Sidd's motion was too awkward, and the table shifted, wobbling with him. The ball-propped paddle on the table clattered down and the ball rolled around the surface while Sidd winced.

The triller he had heard flapped, slurched, and slapped across the upper threshold frame, onto the rec room ceiling. The darkness, cramped position, and trillers' strange attributes made a clear view impossible, but the rec room filled with a sharp funk like brine and bile.

Sidd shuddered, shaking the table, and the ping-pong ball rolled off, tapping repeatedly as it bounced away. The triller stopped climbing and Sidd caught a glimpse as it shifted its body across the ceiling to follow the ball, and Sidd had to close his eyes to keep from losing his mind.

"Duh-Duh-Dusteeee!"

Sidd's eyes snapped open and he almost emptied his bowels. Shaking, he chanced a look.

Granger wasn't dead—not quite, anyway.

When the triller shifted on the ceiling to get a better view of the bouncing ball, it brought the portion of its body that Granger was currently suspended in around closer to Sidd.

Most of his body was burned away, down to exposed bone, organ, and muscle. Part of Granger's head and left shoulder were still outside of the triller's muck.

Then he saw another eye peeking at him, a few feet over on the squirming bone sack mass—Khondji's only remaining eye, stemming out from the last part of his still-human brain.

The one that had grown inside Khondji and taken him over must have fused with this larger one it had called for.

Granger glared down at him through agonized eyes and repeated, "Sih-Siiiiidd!"

Sidd tried to tuck himself even farther into the space under the ping-pong table as he stared at Granger, unable to look away.

The triller didn't seem to approve of Granger's wailing and proceeded to suck him further into its mass of living, murky slime and black bone.

Granger tried to call out to Sidd again but it caught in his throat and his eyes went blank, starting to roll around slowly like that nasty goop had finally eaten its way into his braincase—like it had done to Ojeda.

Sidd closed his eyes and again decided that he just wanted to live long enough to get a drink and maybe some goddamn sleep.

The triller clung to the ceiling for what seemed like ten minutes to Sidd but was probably more like thirty seconds. After letting out a low warble, it clawed, kneaded, and swung itself around on the ceiling before heading out of the rec room, back toward the Air Plant dome it had entered from.

Sidd waited in silence, then slid out from under the table, slung his pack back over his dive-suit and quickly crept to the door where the Staysec troops had caught his attention earlier. The corridor was dark, save for the emergency strips, but seemed empty. He opened the door, stepped through, then closed it behind him.

The trees in the ring corridor looked ominous in the dim glow of the strips, but his eyes adjusted quickly enough that he could stand it.

He followed the corridor a ways, passing the elevator junction they had taken down to the moon pools, continuing on.

Sidd slipped through an open door, scanned the dimly lit interior, then crouch-jogged through a dimly-lit automated cafeteria. He noticed food, drinks, and trays scattered all over. The cooking and cleaning drones were still whirring and clicking about.

A decent sized group had been grabbing a bite when the first trillers found their way up out of the moonpool level and elevator shaft.

Sidd shuddered from thinking about it—then again when he realized he hadn't seen a single body.

He'd caught glimpses of more than enough that turned and twisted his stomach. Things he was almost thankful were only faintly lit. Severed limbs. Spilled organs. Blood had sprayed, splattered, and pooled all over—most of it dried now—but no bodies.

After leaving the cafeteria, he made his way to a familiar set of stairs. As he climbed them, he felt his steps becoming easier and more fluid. The supply workers turned off the para-grav on the loading docks to make work a little easier.

The hatch at the top of the stairs was bent, shuddering, and sliding roughly up and down at a slight angle to its normal path. It was open just enough to crawl under and into a narrow hall with a ceiling that doubled as the loading area floor. Blinking shop lights played across metal stairs at the end of the hall, which ascended to be flush with the dock floor. As Sidd climbed the short set of stairs, he heard trilling.

He crouched as he neared the top of the stairs, keeping his head about level with the loading dock floor. Sidd let his eyes adjust to the dim glow of a few scattered emergency lights.

Without warning the sporadic trilling became a cacophony, and Sidd realized there were even more trillers than he had feared. From the short bursts of vocalizations, he theorized that they were maybe mapping the huge disc of the loading area, and the vertical tunnel that connected it to the surface, with their weird sonar.

Sidd saw a row of resting power loaders in the direction he needed to go, snuck up and out, then bounded softly over to take a knee behind them. It sounded like most of the trillers were above, maybe on the inner surface of the colossal ice cylinder that made up the vertical tunnel or on the securing rings that ran up it every thirty feet to keep its structural integrity.

A stack of large metal crates represented Sidd's next cover spot, and he started bounding toward it, but the trillers all ceased warbling at once, and he panicked—

Sidd slipped on the cold metal surface of the bare dock , sliding on his butt toward the crates, colliding with the lowest, legs up and on his back.

Sidd went stock-still in this awkward missionary position and shook from the fear and cold. He looked straight up into the gaping black maw of the surface tunnel, and he could see fleeting reflections of the forms of a few dozen trillers and faint impressions of more up where it got even darker.

If there were dozens here, how many of them lived down in the ancient machines? Was this all of them, or was it just a larger hunting group?

Sidd gently rolled over into a crouch and started toward the drill-trucks. As he approached a row of three of them, he slowed and tucked himself behind a steel pillar support for the first of a set of rings of platform that lined the tunnel opening above—

There were trillers near the truck.

He looked around for some way to distract the creatures.

There was an automated forklift near him with a pallet of insulated filters on it.

Sidd crept to it and pressed in a manual override command, then setting a destination past the drill-trucks and tapping his finger in air, which created a waypoint in his overlay that the forklift would make its way to.

He took a deep breath and slowly let it out, knowing that once he activated it and got to a truck...things were going to get dicey.

Sidd started the forklift and it shuddered to life, rolling away down its own calculated wayfinding path toward the spot he marked.

The trillers descended, flapping and kneading themselves over to that side, and Sidd stalked over to the row of drill-trucks.

He crept down along a fifteen-foot cylinder of "adaptive" drill on the closest truck and came around the back of an assist-thruster encircled driving compartment on its rear section. He leaned against a wall of ice, bordered by metal supports and keyed a code into a panel on a plasteel-framed bubble of thick plexi making up a good portion of the driver's cabin rear, and the vertical dome broke apart for him.

Sidd climbed into the cabin, unslung his air tube pack, took his hat from the dive suit and put it on. Then he unsealed and took off the top half of the suit, cinched it at the waist, and let the rest drop down.

He took the control seat and secured himself into a four-point harness. Activated and set everything he could on the instrument panels that wouldn't call attention to him.

Shakily grabbed one of two curved vertical booms on each side of the driver's seat—which were topped with inward-facing throttle handles that resembled those on an off-road motorcycle and operated similarly to old tank controls. He slipped his boots into two pedal clamps, which auto tightened.

A display warmed up to a deep blue-black with bright green data and simple geometric symbols, which represented distance and designation. Video feeds from between the navigation tracks and drill also warmed up, and he could see flopping and slapping in the distance as the trillers attacked the still-moving, oblivious fork-lift.

"Good a time as any, I guess."

Sidd slammed the flat of his right fist onto the master starter and the drilling vehicle shuddered, whining up to a low roar. He tried to manually shift it into gear, but the tracks and the drill were going through mandatory startup diagnostics he'd forgotten about.

The thrashing and whipping in the distance slowed as Sidd's heart rate increased. A few of the trillers tentatively approached the noisy, unmoving vehicle.

Sidd felt the diagnostic devices cycle down, pressed a clutch thumb button, and put the truck in gear with a foot pedal. He thrust the controls forward in parallel, sending the drill-truck surging forward across the dock toward the confused trillers.

After Sidd entered a macro he and Granger had come up with on another drunken night, the drill-truck maneuvered into something like a wide, tumbling "drift" to face toward the Tube's ice wall.

He engaged the drill and its heat-assist system as he came out of the curving path of the trick move, and thrust the control booms forward again, driving the drill-truck straight toward the bare patch of ice wall in its frame.

Just before the truck's front end made contact with the ice, the drill reformed into a mean-looking, super-heated toothed cone.

There was some resistance as the drill slid into the thick ice, but it made quick progress. The wide-angle feeds went dark, then infrared green as the drill went deeper. Shaved ice started shooting out of six slit-ports on the outermost ring of the truck's rear. The drill-truck's lowest tracks were still on the slick deck floor, so there was slippage, slowing down Sidd's escape.

Sidd looked back out the plexi bubble, and his blood went cold as he saw several trillers right behind the truck, black bones shifting around inside their sac exteriors.

Orange-blinking PARTIAL TRACTION and grayed out FULL TRACTION were displayed in indicators on his readouts.

"Come on... I just need a few more feet!"

There was a powerful slap and thump behind him, and he whipped his head around to see the bubble mostly obscured by sizzling, pulsing triller.

Sidd fought through a tremor of pure terror, then flipped a toggle with his thumb to lock the left control boom in position. With the same shaking hand, Sid grabbed a T-shaped charging handle to the left of his control dash and pumped it forward and back, pounding a large button—

The aft drill-assist thrusters kicked on, sputtering intensely in a preset pattern around the thruster ring.

The triller flapped and kneaded itself away from the truck and the drill pushed further into the ice. The traction indicator switched to orange-blinking then solid blue, FULL TRACTION, as a circulating claw and curved spike assist system on the track-covered outer-middle surface of the drill-truck gained purchase in the ice. These eager, powerful claws carried the drill-truck into and through the ice much faster than the drill and regular-toothed tracks could on their own. Having finished their burn pattern, the thrusters sputtered out, but the claws were more than enough on their own once engaged, unless an extra "oomph" was needed.

Sidd went straight into the ice for about a hundred feet before he eased the booms back and began his angled ascent. He zigzagged vertically, going toward the Tube tunnel to the surface, then away, then back again.

"This just might work," Sidd said to himself, then winced a bit and licked his chapped, broken lips. He eased the truck up around and toward the tunnel again, and something caught the very edge of his peripheral vision as he leaned into the curve.

Sidd looked back out through the rear bubble and caught something glinting. He flicked a flood-light ring on. The lights surged and flashed—Sidd saw almost a dozen trillers clawing and swinging their way across the freshly made ice tunnel ceiling.

"Oh, this will not do...." Sidd said to himself in approximation of his Indian-Welsh father's calm, soothing voice, belying the terror he was feeling.

Sidd maneuvered the truck up into a higher angle and accelerated, craning his neck to look back again, but saw no sign of trillers.

Then he looked back at his indicators. A warning was blinking. Even in one-eighth Earth gravity, the truck's immense weight could cause serious issues with steep angles. The trillers were too fast—his camping plan was out. And Sidd knew he needed an alternative to the Plug Base.

The Lake?

The Lake!

The Lake was the secondary base—used for studying "chaos terrain" mostly—that he and Granger had discussed what seemed like ages ago.

The scientists kept it pilot-lit just below the ice-surface ceiling of one of hundreds of lakes between the ocean and the ice crust surface of Europa. Sid hit the thrusters again and steered to line up with the Lake base symbol on the display and eased the booms all the way forward.

A flashing caught his eye and he realized it was a thruster warning light just as the thrusters cut out for diagnostics. The drill-truck slowed to a stop and Sidd beat against the panel.

"No!"

After fighting his controls and seething for a moment, Sidd engaged two sets of telescoping spikes—which shot away from the cylindrical trunk of the drill-truck and anchored it stock-still into the ice at almost sixty degrees.

After unbuckling and removing his harness, Sidd balanced himself on the angled driver-chair rig, then let go and fell/floated down to the curved floor around a suit-and-gear compartment. He keyed in a code, and it popped open.

He took a bubble mask from the compartment and secured it over his face, then flipped his hat backwards and pulled the straps over it. Two small air tubes sprouted from the jawline and ran roughly parallel to it. He breathed in and out to prime them.

Next, he pulled out a climbing harness and rope rig and put it on over his half-worn dive suit. Then some skin-tight climbing gloves and a pair of extra ice cleats that he stepped into with a snap, compatible with his dive boots. Two ice axes hung from loops on both sides of the harness's belt.

After hooking his climbing rig to an inch-thick steel ring in the ceiling, Sidd opened the rear bubble hatch and climbed down. He looped his climbing rope onto a support hook and let himself dangle, allowed some more slack, then climbed out and around to the left of the rear thruster and light ring that the triller had briefly attached itself to.

Sidd pulled his left ice axe up from its loop and clicked its handle's base to an attachment at the end of a thick wire spool on the belt. He raised the axe and swung it down into the ice wall nearest him. It went in tight with a thunk, and he pressed a button, taking up most of the slack and giving himself another anchor point while he worked.

Sidd flicked on a light in the upper chest part of the climbing harness and tried to ignore the freshly bored, yawning tunnel of inky black descending at an angle from his perch.

Three of the thrusters were melted and destroyed.

Even still shaking from his ongoing terror and increasing exhaustion, Sidd fell back on his training.

Popping open the casing, he shut off the fuel ports to the thrusters and set them to bypass. He rotated and detached each thruster before letting them slide out of their housings and down onto the steep slope of ice. They slid out of sight, engulfed by the darkness.

In the silence after the scraping was gone, Sidd heard the first trills. They were quiet at first but quickly rose in volume. He pried his ice axe out of its slot in the ice and held its button to release the wire connector and re-hung it from its loop. He was about to climb back around into the bubble when an idea struck him.

Sidd reached back into the thruster housing and detached one of the fuel tubes from its port frame and pulled it out as far as he could. He got it across his chest and a bit more out, then threw the bypass back to its off position, covered the nozzle partially to increase line pressure, and proceeded to spray the tunnel all around like he was watering a lawn with a hose. He concentrated on the curved, angled ceiling of the tunnel.

The trilling and shrieking of black bone claws in ice grew in volume in the dark, and Sidd shuddered as he realized he needed to get out of there.

He flipped the line back to bypass, cutting off its stream and started to climb back around—

Sidd slipped down off the thruster ring, swinging back and forth at the end of his climbing rope.

With all the thick clothing and gloves, he hadn't noticed the thruster fuel from his spraying hand trickling down his body and covering his chest, legs, and boots. The climbing extension hook he'd looped the rope through had him dangling over the angled ice of the tunnel. He was only five or six feet above the slope, but it might as well have been above a bottomless pit if he couldn't get a foothold.

Sidd tried to pull himself up, in hope of gaining some purchase, but his hands slipped from the slickness of the fuel.

He heard the trillers getting closer, and he kept trying to overpower the lubrication on the line, to no avail.

He managed a few feet up the line through shear will, only to slip back down to bob and squirm at the bottom like a worm on a hook.

The trillers were even closer now.

Sidd did the only thing he could think to do—he started to kick and pump his legs. It went impossibly slow at first, but he got himself swinging forward and back at the end of the line. The trilling grew so close that he expected to be engulfed in searing flesh, goop, and piercing black bone at any moment.

"HA!" Sid couldn't help exclaiming as he caught the ice with his cleated boots—but the ice was too slick from the fuel.

"NO!"

He swung back one more time—sure that he was going to get clamped onto any moment—then pumped hard and made it even closer, this time really kicking his boots down into the ice and sticking firm.

Sidd scrambled up the short, steep slope to the thruster ring and climbed up into the drive bubble, hauling himself into the seat—pulling his climbing rig up after him—and slammed the manual bubble control—but just before it could seal, a few trillers kneaded and slapped onto it. Digestive fluid sprayed through the seams. The bubble sealed, but an alarm started flashing and beeping—Sid couldn't worry about that right now.

"Who wants some fried freaky ku-rah-geh?!"

As Sidd started the drill-truck and thrusters back up, the tunnel blasted into a rolling fireball from the fuel he had sprayed all over.

He threw the booms forward and maxed out the thrusters as the fireball quickly extinguished itself in the low atmosphere. He looked back and caught a glimpse of flailing, burning trillers—some tumbling back down the tunnel and others still trying to cling to the tunnel ceiling while their translucent flesh was burned opaque around the boney guts.

The drill-truck bored and climbed back up to almost top-speed, and Sidd watched as the Lake base symbol became larger on the screen.

It hit him then that the creatures would just follow him up into the base if he made a tunnel straight to it. Panicking at not having thought of that, his eyes darted around on the digital representation of the base—and the lake itself.

If he couldn't go straight up to the base, maybe he could make a confusing distraction for the goddamn things—and maybe even flush them back down to "chandelier" station if he was extra lucky.

Sidd changed his angle of climb and steered toward a part of the lakebed that was almost vertical. He was coming up on his penetration point fast, but worried it wouldn't be fast enough.

The drill-truck shuddered and moaned but kept going.

As the drill broke into the lake, the shudder lessened some due to it now swirling water instead of boring into ice. The claws kept cycling, and thrusters kept pushing it further into the resisting body of water.

Sidd felt the resistance in his control booms' weird movements.

He realized all too late that the thrusters were going to cut out as soon as the water hit them and the truck would just become a plug for the tunnel and trap him there. In a panic, he threw the booms in opposite directions, turning the drill-truck with the last bit of traction that he had.

As the drill-truck popped out into the lake in a twisting, angled rotation, the lake water burst violently into the gap between it and the tunnel mouth, dousing the thrusters and sucking the truck down hard against the lake wall with a monumental crunch.

The water poured into the tunnel and the suction of the slowly building vacuum started to drag the drill-truck back toward the tunnel mouth. Sidd frantically looked out through the bubble and watched the tunnel opening grow larger again like a hungry monster's mouth.

Sidd remembered the spikes and rushed to engage them in time. Two sets got almost all their spikes into the steep slope of lakebed ice while the others thrust out into water impotently.

The drill-truck stuck in place and vibrated at the end of their long, thin anchor rods while the rushing water sucked and tugged at it.

Sidd got out of the driver's seat and took his breathing mask off, pulled his dive-suit back up onto his upper body, and tucked his lucky hat back into the chest pocket. He crossed to a compartment and took two climbing axes out of it, securing them in loops on his suit's waist.

Then he sealed the suit and activated its helmet.

After his helmet sealed and before he could think too long about it, he bypassed the pressure-seal system—which was already breached and leaking from the triller attack, forming a growing pool. The bubble broke apart, and the lake water rushed in. He braced himself for the impact but not well enough—

The rising wall of freezing water slammed him back against the circular monitor and instruments.

Sidd fought off the powerful chill and reached through the water, grabbing the headrest of the driver's chair, then pulled himself off the dash. He forced himself through the driver's compartment and stopped at the open bubble.

He grabbed handholds on the thruster and light ring, climbed out of the open bubble, and onto the rear rings of outer tractor teeth. He progressed from hold to hold and teeth to spikes until he was climbing the drill toward the upward-curving ice wall of the lakebed.

Sidd took out the ice axes—ice-climbing in the draining contents of an enormous sink. He thought about trying the dive-suit thrusters, but they were designed for climbing the domes with their magnetic effect. He'd probably just get thrown around in the water and sucked down the tunnel too.

He slammed down the first axe and advanced off the drill, bringing the other down before pulling out the first, and so on. Sidd made progress up the ice wall despite the constant suction of the water trying to pull him back down to his tunnel.

About a hundred feet up the wall from the drill-truck and tunnel mouth, Sid took a short rest with both axes and boots in the ice as anchors. He looked down toward the tunnel mouth and jolted, almost losing grip on his axes and footholds—

The trillers were fighting the suction and kneading and flapping their way up out of the tunnel.

Sidd started climbing again, and fast. As he climbed, the water became brighter and clearer, and he realized there was a surface now that he could reach. He kept pushing and reached the surface, climbing up out of the lake water. The minimal gravity replaced the lake's suction.

Dark shapes moving down in the water kept Sidd from slowing, driving him ever higher even through his fatigue and the burning in his muscles. He kept climbing toward the ice crust ceiling of the lake chamber—chaotically crushed together like icebergs holding each other up from horizontal pressure.

Sidd saw the glow from a frost-covered viewport wall on part of the Lake base above him. He climbed for it, but, as he ascended toward an overhang—that he mistakenly took for a natural hole in the ice wall—he realized it was a moon pool opening that had until recently opened onto water. After calculating the chances of climbing up into a bad situation, he changed course to climb up to it.

As Sidd carefully climbed up through the ovular moon pool opening, he heard trills from below and looked down to see his hunters surfacing and climbing the ice at speed in their weird ways.

Using a support bar intended for climbing in and out of the water of the lake, Sidd hauled himself up into the dive room of the Lake facility. He scrambled for a control panel near the moon pool and engaged the hatch-close command. A heavy oval of thick steel rotated onto the moon pool, opening on articulated hydraulic hinges and clamped down on a thick rubber oval gasket.

On a panel near the hatch control, Sidd engaged the pressure system to rebalance the room, but not for the intended purpose—he needed a perimeter alarm.

Sidd popped his helmet and hurried through the dark Lake base to the comms room, only to find the equipment gutted and a printed paper sign that read:

WORKING ON IT -GRANGER.

In his own roundabout way, Granger had taken revenge on Sidd for not being able to save him.

THIRTEEN

Sidd collapsed to his knees, defeated.

That was it…. There's no other options. Might as well just—

Then he remembered the subsurface tram to the Plug base. Comms might still be working there.

He stood, put his hat back on, and hurried through the base to the Plug tram.

Once he reached the tram docking station, he called for it.

Sidd was able to watch a visual representation of its progress with a glowing line and little animated icon. It seemed much longer to Sidd but in only about two minutes, it had reached the ¾ hashmark on the display—

ABORTED

ABORTED

RETURNING TO PLUG BASE

"Wait…No!"

A feed flicked into view in the peripheral of his AR overlay. It was Vanlint's feed, this time the view was darker with only hints of tunnels and structures, like she had descended into the fissure below the alien machines—or possibly even into the huge obscured area that the equipment implied was present under the icy sea floor.

A little circular feed faded up in the corner of her larger feed, a view of her face in a mask of concentration as she piloted her mini-sub.

-I'm afraid I can't...—w you to leave, Mr. Priddy.-

"What the actual fuck are you on about?!"

-The station ha...—en placed under full quarantine. Commu...—ns totally disabled. No one com...—or out until a special heavy-weapons assisted c...—nment and research team arrives.-

"You knew.... You did this!"

Sidd saw the frequency numbers change on the feed's info panel and Vanlint sounded a bit clearer.

-Not exactly, no. I left before this happened and was unaware they had found the station. I had no intention of this occurring. I was aware of it, though, by the time I contacted Khondji when he was with you.-

"But you blocked all our comms. Made it impossible for Staysec or anyone else to organize a defense...."

-You are far more intelligent than you let on, aren't you? Yes, that was my doing. I assure you, the footage gathered of the creatures' abilities and tactics will be put to good use.-

"Why? Why did you...?"

-You saw this for yourself. This structure is.... I don't have the words to describe it. We have found remnants of this civilization's machines and equipment before, but those really were ruins. These are almost fully functional, albeit malfunctioning strangely. Possibly causing the creation of those predatory creatures.-

"What do you mean?"

-It's only a hypothesis...but I think those machines were part of the power infrastructure for an alien research or observation station. If I will allow myself an educated stretch...whatever power source they were using may have been prone to instability.-

"And it melted down or somethin' and those things used to be the alien... people?"

-In the beginning. This is a truly ancient site. Possibly enough that the creatures we are dealing with have evolved from those original mutated lifeforms.-

"Yeah, real goddamn fascinatin'—and worth the lives of a few thousand human beings so you can get some research data?!"

-Oh please, Mr. Priddy. I had little hope of finding anything here. Ruins. Artifacts. This? For this find, I would have sacrificed millions.-

Sidd studied her face and knew she meant it.

"When those things get bored up here, they're gonna come back home and find you down there eatin' their porridge. And after they pry your tin can open, I hope you feel every second of them digesting you."

Sidd deactivated his comms completely.

"Well...you all gonna come get some din-din?!"

All Sidd got in reply was a distant sound of moaning, creaking metal and plasteel. That was followed immediately by his alarm—pressure loss and integrity breach claxons and monotone-voiced warnings.

He considered using Vanlint's code to bring the tram back, but with her attention on him, he knew she'd figure it out and lock him out or change it, effectively causing the same result.

Sidd's eyes darted back and forth as he waited for the creatures to find him.

His eyes landed on a small plastic model of a corporate competitor's atmosphere processor, and Sidd's new plan slammed him in the chest.

Olatunji-Huang were on this moon somewhere, from what Vanlint had said herself in what seemed like forever ago now—and they were almost definitely far better armed and equipped. Kintetsu was a huge corporation, but O-H was the biggest deal around.

"I'm gonna defect..." he said to himself.

Sidd rushed through the base to its loading area and found no drill-trucks, but there were a few enclosed, shielded snowmobiles—used for the rare and short surface research missions. They consisted of a two-person-wide ball of thick, one-way reflective plexi with a seven-foot high, round-edged rectangle ten-foot long of thick, heavily shielded plasteel jutting back from it with a hatch on the rear. The tracks were below the cylinder with two steering skis resting below the driver's ball on articulated suspension.

After popping the seal on the right side of the closest snowmobile's ball compartment, Sid took his ice axes from their loops and threw them in the interior of the cylinder.

Sidd unsealed and tore off his dive-suit, grabbing a thicker surface suit from a wall peg and halfway put it on, securing the waist area with the suit's self-sizing internal belt.

The suits were about four or five inches thick and—other than an embedded bulb of air tank in the small of the back—all insulation and shielding. They didn't even have helmets—just big, puffy hoods that came up from the back and over the entire head to seal into the chest. A rebreather piece fit into the wearer's mouth, and a small curved screen was installed where an eye panel would be on a normal suit, sending the feed from cameras on the suit's outer hood.

Trilling—and closer than he was expecting.

Sidd climbed in and sealed the thick door next to him. Then pulled a swiveling control wheel over to his side and quickly spun a dynamo handle on the side of his seat to prime a starter system. He started the snowmobile, drove it toward a huge surface lift in the far wall of the loading area and keyed in a remote activation command into a panel.

ACCESS DENIED

QUARANTINE IN PLACE

"Fuck!"

He thought for a few seconds, then keyed in Vanlint's code and prayed she didn't realize she'd sent it to anyone but Khondji.

It worked!

But the trillers also reached the loading area as the lift doors were opening. Sidd gunned it inside.

He frantically jabbed the CLOSE and LIFT commands into the panel. The doors started closing—but the trillers were too fast and made it into the lift.

Sidd stifled his panic and drove the powerful snowmobile in

figure eights and donuts around the twenty-five-hundred-square-foot floor of the climbing lift, succeeding in throwing off the trillers the few times they were able to get hold.

The lift stopped and the doors opened on the powerfully serene surface of Europa—spindly rust-colored fissures miles across and craggy, broken hills and shelves of ice with flats ranging from dark-blue obsidian to opaque white and gray expanses in-between. Jupiter loomed, huge and almost bisected by the horizon. Io cruised lazily through the space between the moon Sidd was on and the huge planet both of them revolved around. Space and stars filled the rest of his view, and the distant sun looked like a speck compared to the view of it from Earth that Sidd remembered.

The bulk of the tenuous all-oxygen atmosphere of Europa wouldn't reach a person's waist on a good day, so the surface was eerily quiet above that level as Sidd burst out from the lift interior and tore across the surface in his growling vehicle.

He was thankful for the sound inside the sealed snowmobile because the extreme quiet of the surface would be too much for him to handle right then.

As he was driving the fast, nimble machine over the ice, Sidd keyed in a sensor search that he hoped would reveal O-H bases. From his take on the readings, there were two—but the closest was behind him.

"Shit!"

Sidd altered his course, steering the snowmobile back toward the lake in as wide an arc as he could manage. He maneuvered through a gap between some craggy chaos terrain and started across a smooth expanse of translucent white-blue ice over the lake.

The part he was on must've been a different chamber of the greater lake area, because he could see water below through varying thicknesses of the ice—and trillers!

Several of the creatures paced his progress across the ice surface by kneading and surging through the water below.

A rear-image feed showed several more still on his tail across the surface as well—and they were gaining.

Sidd had hit top speed already and hoped against hope he

could make it somehow, while knowing he wouldn't.

Even in his haze of panic and fear, he still noticed a few of the trillers below the ice breaking away and easily "swimming" into the distance, out of sight.

Splitting his attention between the trillers below the lake ice and the ones closing the distance behind him, Sid didn't notice the ice ahead collapsing until just before he reached it.

Bastards laid a trap!

Sidd tried to steer to the side of the sizzling, sinking ice and almost succeeded—but caught the edge of the opening hole and the snowmobile teetered for a moment before slamming sideways onto the ice and sliding to a stop thirty feet further across the surface.

The surface trillers reached the snowmobile just as Sidd was pulling the rest of his surface suit up over and sealing everything into place around himself. It took a moment for his suit view screen to warm up, and he almost hyperventilated waiting to see again.

He felt the trillers striking and sizzling into the outer surface of the immobile vehicle before the panel warmed up and saw parts of them through the front and rear plexis.

One of the monsters attached itself to the outer surface of the driver's ball. As its juices melted the plexi, Sidd backed into the cylinder only to find another creature sizzling against the rear plexi. He shifted away from it, and his right hand came down on an axe.

Sidd grabbed the handles and raised them. He rose into a crouch and looked back and forth, gauging which plexi would capitulate first.

The winner was the driver's ball, its surface finally giving way like that foam eaten by acetone he remembered.

Sidd closed his eyes for a moment and pictured Granger, Ojeda, Asaaluk, and the others—but mostly, Granger—before opening them again and readying his primitive weapons. He tried his hardest to muster a war cry, but it was muffled by his suit mouthpiece and cracked in his throat. A distant part of him that wasn't terrified and amped up by all the adrenaline felt ridiculous.

The rear plexi gave way too, but the triller on the ball was trying to wriggle its way in, tentacles and bone-spikes and talons whipping and cutting the air near him, so he tried to focus on where to strike at it.

Sidd knew he had no chance...but he waited with his heart pumping hard in his chest, axes raised in shaking gloved hands.

Then the trillers seemed to slow their prying and swiping.

They changed to a squealing and fluttering and after a few more seconds, stopped.

Sidd forced himself to look toward the rear plexi, and what he saw made him crouch and gawk.

The trillers at the snowmobile rear had collapsed to the ice surface and were pulsating languidly. He looked to the ball in front and saw the one that had been lashing out at him was in the same state, as was another that must have dropped off the snowmobile from above.

Sidd didn't move again until all of the trillers' movement had stopped. He dreaded the moment when they would spring back to life...but that hadn't come.

After getting up and cautiously moving to the rear plexi, he nudged the triller against its base out of the way through the holes it had melted in it, then keyed its OPEN command.

As he was crawling out of the snowmobile, he saw that the trillers' gooey masses had a boiled look to their insides now, and it occurred to Sidd that direct and prolonged exposure to the radiation pelting the surface due to such minimal atmosphere must have "cooked" them.

There were trillers below his boots that he could see through a few feet of lake surface ice, just watching him from farther down. They must have figured out what had happened to their chums, or felt Jupiter's scorching radiation for themselves.

Sidd started laughing and couldn't stop for a moment, then he crouched and yelled through his thick face covering and his breathing mouthpiece, "You go back down to Hell, you fuckin' demon bastards! And tell Vanlint to kiss my insignificant ass!"

He stomped down at their vague forms in the ice and laughed, but saw cracks forming and stopped.

With a decent effort he eventually succeeded at righting the snowmobile, which appeared to still be intact enough for transportation. He climbed into the breezy, open cabin and settled in the driver's seat. He primed and started it, then throttled it some to test it out. Worked well enough.

Sidd throttled up harder and started across the ice once again, this time with no creatures in pursuit—at least none that were inclined to attack or harry him further. The trillers were no doubt pacing him in the water under the ice, but he would be across the lake and onto solid ice again soon and alone with only his thoughts.

At first the idea of defecting seemed distant and a little guilt-inducing. Now, he was thankful that he just might survive long enough to do it.

Sidd just hoped that Kintetsu's cloaked competitors hadn't made any similar life-form discoveries of their own.

And if he got off this nightmare factory of a moon and made it to a nice terraformed planet—or even got back to Earth itself—he was never leaving its atmosphere again.

ABOUT THE AUTHOR

Patrick Loveland is an author, screenwriter, and artist. By day, he works at a state college in Southern California, where he lives with his wife, young daughter, and a big, black, maniacally chittering cat. Patrick's stories have appeared in anthologies and periodicals published by April Moon Books, Shadow Work Publishing, EyeCue Productions, Bold Venture Press, Sirens Call Publications, Indie Authors Press, PHANTAXIS, and the award-winning Crime Factory zine. Patrick's first (now out-of-print) novel, A Tear in the Veil, was published in 2017 by April Moon Books (to be re-released in the future under its working title, FIFTYONEFIFTY). His first short story collection (including its titular novella) TOO MANY EYES and Other Thrilling Strange Tales was released in 2019.

Explore the darker sides of your world at

WWW.DARKERWORLDS.ORG

Made in the USA
Middletown, DE
21 September 2023

38928607R00080